THEIR FIRST KISS

He was so strong, so handsome—a man any woman would love. While she let her gaze travel over his entire face, Rand's gray eyes never left her mouth. And finally, as she knew he would, he bent his head and claimed her lips.

On the instant, she was lost in the warmth and passion of his kiss. With her heart pounding madly against her ribs, she felt her limbs lose their power to bear her weight, forcing her to lean against him for support. The moment she relaxed, he deepened the kiss, and eons later, when he lifted his head, Harriet was weak with sensation.

She could not move. She could not breathe. All she could do was feel, delighting in his every caress. . . .

Miss Wilson's Reputation

Martha Kirkland

A SIGNET BOOK

SIGNET
Published by New American Library, a division of
Penguin Putnam Inc., 375 Hudson Street,
New York, New York 10014, U.S.A.
Penguin Books Ltd, 80 Strand,
London WC2R 0RL, England
Penguin Books Australia Ltd, Ringwood,
Victoria, Australia
Penguin Books Canada Ltd, 10 Alcorn Avenue,
Toronto, Ontario, Canada M4V 3B2
Penguin Books (N.Z.) Ltd, 182–190 Wairau Road,
Auckland 10, New Zealand

Penguin Books Ltd, Registered Offices:
Harmondsworth, Middlesex, England

First published by Signet, an imprint of New American Library,
a division of Penguin Putnam Inc.

First Printing, May 2002
10 9 8 7 6 5 4 3 2 1

To Miss Rachel Lynn Gormley,
and to all the other young people who
find it difficult to go into the world
on a daily basis. God bless you all.

Chapter One

London
March, 1815 . . .

Randolph Dunford, the sixth Baron Dunford, was bored. In truth, he had been bored for the better part of six months, ever since his return to England. If anything was guaranteed to cure a man of his ennui, however, it was walking alone in the frosty predawn hours and spying two roughly dressed men skulking behind the wall of the corner townhouse.

"Damnation," he muttered. It was not as if he had never been waylaid before. In fact, he knew all too well the beatings waiting for a man foolish enough to walk alone on the docks of Barbados, or near the stews of London. It was just that he had not been expecting such a threat in the rather prosaic streets of Marylebone.

Because most of the inhabitants of the area were prosperous cits—men who rose early each day to engage in commerce in the City—these streets were usually deserted after midnight. Not so that morning, and before Rand had time to whistle for a hackney, hoping one of the carriages for hire might be close by, the two knaves rushed toward him. One of them, a large, burly sort with malice in his eyes, held a leather-covered cudgel in his hand, while his accomplice, a short, wiry fellow, held a knife raised and ready for attack.

"Stand back!" Rand ordered. "I am no lamb for the fleecing. If you think I will not fight, you are very much mistaken."

He might just as well have saved his breath, for the smaller man ran swift as a hare and was on him in an instant. Unarmed save for his ebony cane, Rand used the stick to deflect the first broad sweep of the knife. Then, ignoring completely the British code of fair play, he thrust the silver head of the cane between the man's knees and brought the cane up sharply.

As he knew it would, the blow connecting with such a sensitive spot proved most effective. The malefactor cried out in surprise and pain. Half a second later, he bent double and collapsed to the pavement, holding the injured portion of his anatomy. While he groaned in agony, the burly fellow arrived, swung the cudgel, and struck Rand on the left side of his face. Immediately, fireworks went off inside his head, and the metallic taste of blood filled his mouth.

The larger man, ignoring the sound of retching coming from his accomplice, bent down and snatched up the knife. In that moment, Rand, well aware that this might be his only chance for survival, raised his cane and struck the giant a blow to the back of the neck that felled him like a tree.

With both thugs on the ground, Rand staggered back several paces, hoping to regain his equilibrium before either of the miscreants recovered theirs and obliged him to defend himself further. Using the sleeve of his evening coat, he swiped at the blood that ran from his temple to his chin, all the while considering his options. Should he remain here and give these two more of what they deserved? Or should he do the sensible thing and escape while he could?

A sensible man would retrace his steps the two blocks that would take him back to the townhouse of his latest mistress. Rand had left that particular soiled dove after only fifteen minutes in her cloyingly perfumed company, finding her overzealous kisses, interspersed with a renewed bid for yet another piece of jewelry, too tedious to endure. Even so, confronting an angry mistress had to be preferable to being murdered in the street.

Not at all certain that was true, Rand was still vacillating between the sensible approach and his admittedly pagan desire to show those two thugs the error of their ways, when he realized that either choice might be beyond his present capabilities. The blow from the cudgel had left him dizzy and as weak as a kitten. As well, his ears rang, and spots of various colors floated before his eyes.

To allow his vision time to clear, he leaned for a moment upon the iron handrail of the stairs that led to the kitchen area of the modest, codestone townhouse. While he stood thus, his head down, he heard the unmistakable scrape of an iron bolt being pulled back. Within seconds, the entry door to the townhouse was swung open, and the light from a small lamp pooled on the steps.

"Come inside quickly," someone urged him, "before those footpads recover their senses."

Rand was not at all certain who was speaking to him, except that the voice was feminine and youngish. Not that it mattered. At that moment, he would have accepted assistance from the devil himself. And why should he not? He and Satan were on intimate terms; they had been for most of Rand's adult life.

Whatever the actual identity of the person with the lamp, she hurried down the three steps and slipped her arm around Rand's waist. In a no-nonsense tone that brooked no refusal, she said, "Lean on me, sir. And please, no arguments."

Since refusing her offer was the last thing on Rand's mind, he draped his arm across her shoulders, noting as he did so that those shoulders were soft, and that the woman smelled fresh and sweet, as though she had not been long from her bath. He let her lead him up the stairs and into her townhouse, then leaned against the wall while she closed the door and shot home the bolt.

"Oh," she said, after turning and getting her first good look at his bloodied face, "you are injured."

"Only a little, I assure you. Certainly not as badly as I might have been save for your courage in coming to my rescue."

The woman paid little attention to what he said. Instead, she slipped her arm around his waist once again. "If you can walk just a bit farther, sir, to the workroom at the rear of the house, I can attend to your injuries there without disturbing the rest of the household."

Workroom? Was she a seamstress, then? Or perhaps a milliner? Rand was surprised, for from her speech, he had thought her a lady of quality.

"I witnessed what happened from my bedchamber window," she said. "You were very quick, sir. And very fortunate. When I saw those men, and realized one of them had a knife, I feared you would be killed. I thank heaven that you were not."

That anyone should care if he lived or died was such a singular experience for Rand that he could not think how to reply. Fortunately, his rescuer did not appear to expect any comment from him, so while they crossed the green-and-gray marble tiles of the small vestibule, he was free to concentrate on the Herculean task of putting one foot in front of the other.

They continued down a short, narrow corridor to the rear of the house, where she opened a door and led him into a largish chamber. It did, indeed, fit the description of a workroom, though the wooden shelves that lined the east and west walls suggested it had probably served at one time as a gentleman's library. The rear wall housed the fireplace and two large windows, and the front wall contained storage cabinets and a door that probably led to the front parlor.

Happy to know his walking was at an end, Rand slipped his arm from around the woman and leaned both his hands on an ancient oak library table that took pride of place in the center of the room. Atop the badly scarred and blotched oak surface stood two beautifully wrought silver candelabra, their branches filled with half-spent beeswax candles. In addition to the lovely silver was a rough wooden workbox, not unlike those carried by carpenters, and a large metal tray that contained what looked like miniature soldering tools, including iron tongs and the sort of thick leather gloves worn by blacksmiths.

At the right corner of the table, someone had affixed two iron pipes about ten inches long and about as big around as a man's thumb. The pipes were fitted together in an L shape whose opening pointed upward, while a third pipe led from the table down to an ironstone cylinder that sat on the floor. Upon the cylinder were printed the words, "Caution. Flammable." Surprised to see such a potentially dangerous container inside a home, Rand was relieved to observe something that looked like it might be a cut-off valve at the neck of the cylinder.

Whatever went on in this workroom, it certainly had nothing to do with such feminine occupations as sewing and millinery. As well, there was a slightly sulphurous smell in the air that made Rand wonder if he had been hit harder than he realized. If so, could this be the pass-through to the netherworld?

Using her foot, which was clad in a homely brown carpet slipper, the woman pulled a plain wooden stool from beneath the table. "Sit here," she said, "while I fetch a basin of water and the medicine box."

Still weak, Rand was more than happy to be seated. He watched while the woman lit the candles, then followed her progress as she took the lamp and crossed to the far side of the room. Between the bookshelves was a door that appeared to give access to the kitchen stairs. After opening that door, she turned back to look at Rand, as if having just remembered something. "Forgive me, sir, but I must ask you not to touch anything in the room."

"No, no. Of course not. I shall sit here, meek as a lamb, and await your return."

"A lamb?" The corners of her mouth twitched, but she schooled her lips before they actually smiled. "You forget, sir, that I witnessed the attack on your person. And having been privy to the deftness with which you dispatched those two felons, I somehow doubt that meekness plays any great part in the makeup of your character."

Not certain he liked being so easy to read, he laid the ebony cane on the table, then made a show of folding his hands and placing them in his lap. Striving for a credible imitation of a sheep, he said, "Baa."

This time she did smile. Not that his gaze remained overlong on her face, for his attention had been caught by her attire. The colored spots were fast disappearing from his vision, and with the extra light from the candles, he realized for the first time that his benefactress was dressed for bed. Her thick brown hair was fashioned into a loose braid that hung down her slender back, and she wore nothing more than a virginal-looking night rail and a plain lawn wrapper.

Remembering that he might well owe this woman his life, he had the grace to refrain from ogling her and turned instead to give the articles on the table a more intense perusal. He heard her descend the stairs, and when she returned several minutes later, she carried a washbasin, a snowy white towel, and a tin box.

By that time, Rand's vision had cleared sufficiently for him to see that she was a handsome woman. Not beautiful, perhaps, not in the accepted mode. And yet, there was something undeniably attractive in the arrangement of her features.

He guessed her age at twenty-five or -six, for her face had traded the plumpness of youth for the more dramatic contours of a fully grown woman. Like her hair, her eyebrows were the color of hot chocolate diluted with only a drop of cream. As for her eyes, she lowered her lids too quickly for him to discern if the irises were brown or green.

Her nose was small and straight, and her complexion was satiny smooth. Rand could not decide, however, if the soft pink tint of her cheeks was always there, or merely the evidence that she knew he was scrutinizing her. To take his mind off her mouth, which was full, the lips soft and well shaped, he said, "May I know your name, Mrs. . . ."

He paused to give her time to respond, but to his surprise, she declined to answer.

She had set the basin on the worktable, and was busy unbuckling the leather strap that secured the tin box containing the medicines. "You will forgive me, sir, but considering the unusual circumstances of our meeting, I think it best that you do not know my name. Nor do I wish you to offer me yours."

"But, ma'am, surely there is no need for such secrecy? I am far too much in your debt to bandy your name about."

"Be that as it may," she replied, withdrawing several sticking plasters and a glass pot containing a foul-smelling balm, "you must allow me to know best."

After dampening the towel, she took his chin in her hand, gently turned his face toward the light, then began to bathe the blood from his wounds. Her touch was light, and her careful, tender strokes such a rarity in Rand's experience that he closed his eyes to shut out all senses save the one of feel.

"You have sustained two cuts, sir, and though I do not think either wound is deep enough to leave a scar, you may wish to consult a physician on the matter first thing tomorrow."

Physicians be damned. As far as Rand was concerned, he could have remained in that room forever, allowing this stranger with the gentle touch to administer to him.

Offering no further comment, his ministering angel applied dabs of the balm, which smelled suspiciously of tar, to a spot just below his eye and to another spot at the edge of his mouth. While she affixed the sticking plasters, he asked if she would reconsider her decision and tell him her name. "I merely wish to know to whom I owe my gratitude for this act of kindness."

"You owe me nothing, sir. Except your promise of complete silence."

As though realizing that he had questions, she said, "I am obliged to earn my living, sir, and though I am in the happy position of being able to work at something I love to do, every coin has two sides. For a woman pursuing my particular sort of occupation," she added, "the reverse side of the coin is that an unsullied reputation is more precious than gold."

Rand was about to suggest that she might be seeing danger where none actually existed, but she obviously read his mind. "Being a man, you cannot be expected to understand my circumstances. However, you may believe me when I tell you that with but a single slip of the tongue you could rob me of my reputation and my livelihood."

She smiled then, as if to take the sting from her next words. "I cannot think, sir, that you would repay my kindness, as you called it, by obliging me to move from this comfortable home directly into the poorhouse."

"No, ma'am, I would not."

"That is good of you. And now," she said, returning the balm pot to the tin box, "since I believe strong spirits are not recommended for a person who has sustained a head injury, may I offer you a cup of tea?"

Though Rand would have been happy to take his chances with a glass of brandy, he agreed to the tea. "It sounds wonderful, ma'am. If it would not be too much trouble."

"No trouble at all." After tucking the medicine box beneath her arm, she gathered up the towel and basin, crossed the room once again, and took the stairs down to the kitchen area.

Aware that the brewing of tea would require several minutes, Rand decided to walk through the door that led to the front parlor. His purpose was twofold: He wanted to test his steadiness, and he wanted to have a look out the front window, to see if his assailants had quit the area.

If the workroom was not what he had expected, the front parlor definitely came as a surprise. Small and sparsely furnished, half the space of the room was taken up by a glass display case about waist high. The light from the distant candles was sufficient for him to see the case, but not strong enough to allow him to inspect the contents. Not that he was all that interested. His primary objective was the window.

Stepping between two brocade-covered wing chairs, the only true furniture in the room, he pushed aside the heavy window hangings and looked out into the street. All was quiet. The two men were gone, and not even the silk evening hat he had lost in the scuffle remained in evidence.

Of Antoine de la Croix—slave trader, pirate, and supposed indigo planter—there was not the first sign. The man had said he would come, that he would have his revenge, and Rand took the man and the threat seriously. The scion of an illustrious family of French émigrés, de la Croix's besetting sin was his pride, and the way the Frenchman saw it, Rand had caused him to lose face.

Gazing down on the empty street, Rand decided that for this evening at least, his sworn enemy had not come. Not sure if he was relieved or disappointed, Rand let the window hangings fall into place. As he turned to go back to the workroom, he accidentally bumped against the display case, and when he did so, something that had stood on the glass surface fell to the floor.

Thankfully, the floor was carpeted, for when he retrieved the fallen item, he discovered it was a miniature silver easel, handsomely wrought and delicately filigreed. Since a dozen calling cards were scattered about on the floor as well, Rand had no trouble discerning the purpose for the easel.

After setting the pretty object back where it belonged, then arranging the calling cards like an artist's canvas in progress, he removed one of the pasteboard squares and took it back to the worktable. Holding the small card up to the light, he read two engraved lines.

MISS HARRIET J. WILSON
KNOWLEDGEABLE IN ALL FORMS OF FINE JEWELRY

Unable to believe the testimony of his eyes, Rand read the lines through a second time. There was no mistake; his sight was not playing him false. The name on the card was, indeed, that of the country's most celebrated courtesan, Harriet Wilson.

Why is Harriet Wilson here? In Marylebone of all places? In this bastion of respectable cits? Had she relatives in the house? Did such women have relatives? Surely they must have had them at one time, for even courtesans did not spring full grown from the head of Zeus, as it were. Perhaps she was visiting incognito. Was that the reason for the plain night-clothes and for her wish to remain anonymous?

To Rand, only one explanation offered itself; the fates were making a May game of him again. Why else would he be set upon by footpads, then granted this particular rescuer?

Not that he had ever met the so-called "Queen of the Demimonde" before this evening. During the months he had been in town, that particular soiled dove was said to be on a repairing lease in the country. Still, her reputation was legendary. And rightly so, for she was the most popular Cyprian of the nineteenth century.

He had heard it said that Harriet Wilson was a woman of rare charm, and since she had been under the protection of several very intelligent and well-placed gentlemen, Rand could believe all that was said of her. Even so, he had not expected a woman of her calling to behave in so genteel a manner, nor to employ such educated speech.

In truth, he quite admired his rescuer, for she had shown uncommon courage in coming to his aid. At the time of the rescue, her willingness to overlook her immodest attire in favor of administering to a wounded man had won her Rand's approval. Now, of course, aware of her true identity, he decided it was likely that she had not given her attire a thought. Certainly not as much as he had when he had observed the feminine curves only hinted at beneath the chaste, unadorned cotton!

He read the calling card again and chuckled at the second line. Knowledgeable in all forms of fine jewelry. The woman had a sense of humor.

Considering the amount of jewelry women of her stamp had gotten out of him in the months since his return to England, Rand could only imagine the number of baubles and geegaws a woman of Harriet Wilson's charm and intelligence must possess. In fact, he was not averse to adding a nice trinket to her collection, in gratitude for her kindness. For that, and for anything else she might consider bestowing upon him before sending him on his way. After all, when she had told him that she was obliged to earn her living, she had added that she was in the happy position of being able to work at something she loved to do. No reason why she should not enjoy it as well.

Not surprisingly, the prospect of a few hours spent in those soft arms was having a decidedly positive effect upon Rand's health. His vigor all but reborn, he was considering the purchase of a diamond clip to adorn her lovely brown hair, when she appeared at the door once more. This time, she carried a plain wooden tray bearing cups, saucers, and a small teapot from which emanated a pleasantly spicy fragrance. To his amusement, she had donned a cook's oversized apron that reached from her shoulders all the way to her ankles, effectively covering the night rail and wrapper.

Rand allowed his gaze to travel slowly over her curvaceous figure, from her head down to her toes, then back up again. When she blushed, as if unaccustomed to such attention, he laughed aloud. "The apron is a nice touch, my dear, but it has come a bit late. The horse has, as they say, already left the stable."

As if surprised by his words, she stared at him, her eyes wide. "Sir, I do not know what you mean by—"

"Come, come, sweetings. Do not spoil what promises to be a lovely encounter by feigning missishness. Believe me, there is no need for pretense between us, *Miss Wilson.*"

Harriet gasped. How had the man learned her name? As long as he had not known who she was, she had felt secure. She had offered him the safety of her house because she could not do otherwise. He was a human being, and she could not stand by and watch him be murdered.

Now, however, she wished she had not been standing at her bedchamber window at just the moment of the attack. For all she knew, the man she had brought into her home could prove to be a blackmailer. With almost no effort on his part, he could ruin her—ruin her good name and with it her business.

His very presence was a threat to her livelihood and to the lives of all those who depended upon her, and that knowledge caused her hands to tremble. Afraid she would drop the tray and wake the household, she hurried over to the worktable. "How . . . How do you know my name?"

Smiling as if this was all an amusing jest, he tapped his chin with one of her calling cards.

The moment her hands were free, Harriet snatched the pasteboard square from his fingers. "Where did you get this?"

"Does it matter, pretty one?"

"Do not call me that!"

"Why should I not? It is no more than the truth. Actually, you are quite lovely. Far lovelier than I had expected." He leaned toward her, his gray eyes alight with flirtatious amusement. "Surely I am not the first man to tell you that you are an altogether lovely and desirable woman?"

To Harriet's dismay, he reached out his hand, ran the tips of his long, well-shaped fingers down the side of her cheek, then tipped her chin up so he could look directly into her eyes. "Nice," he said. "Very nice." At the softly uttered words, warmth skittered up her spine.

"They are green," he said, "with flecks of gold and brown. I had wondered."

"You had?"

"They are like the loveliest of pansies," he added quietly, "all velvety soft and beautiful."

Harriet's breath caught in her throat. No man had ever said such sweet words to her, and like a moth unable to elude the flame, she could not turn away from the warmth of his gaze. She stared into his rugged, rather uncompromising face, his extra height obliging her to tilt her head back. All but mesmerized by his continued touch, and by the masculine, slightly woodsy scent that beguiled its way to her nostrils, she watched unmoving while his head bent and he brushed his lips against hers.

The contact was unimaginably soft, and it lasted mere seconds, but Harriet felt the heat of it spread throughout her entire body. And from the slow smile that tugged at the corners of his mouth, the man knew exactly what that kiss had done to her.

He possessed the devil's own smile, and like his kiss, that smile sent a shaft of awareness through Harriet that made her knees feel as boneless as a rag doll's. Worse yet, her traitorous body whispered softly to her, encouraging her to lean toward the man whose lips had bewitched hers, to see if a second kiss might prove even sweeter.

She did not lean forward, of course, and several moments passed before she came to her senses and realized that as a respectable female she should be boxing his ears as he deserved. She should be telling him in no uncertain terms that she detested him for his unprincipled behavior and for his careless employment of that devilish smile and that kiss.

And yet, she said nothing. Honesty compelled her to wonder if it was actually him she detested, or was it herself, for her response to that smile? That feathery soft kiss?

Not certain she wanted to know the answer, she vowed that the next time she rescued a man from a pair of footpads, she would check first to see that he was old, ugly, and completely without charm. As a woman who prided herself on her wisdom and the practicality of her decisions, she had behaved uncharacteristically foolish from the very beginning. She should have considered all the ramifications before rushing out into the night to rescue a gentleman whose coat fit his broad shoulders to perfection and whose pewter-gray eyes had a smoky, mysterious quality to them, as though they hid secrets best left unrevealed.

Girding herself in a protective cloak of indignation, she slapped his hand away from her chin. "How dare you kiss me! Sir, you are no gentleman."

"That is a given, Miss Wilson. Not that I expected such a deficiency to matter overmuch to the famous Harriet Wilson. Or should I say the *infamous* Harriet Wilson?"

Infamous? Harriet groaned, for now she understood.

The heat of embarrassment crept up her neck. He thought she was Harriette Wilson. She should have guessed as much, for it was not the first time her name had been confused with that of the notorious courtesan.

"Sir! I am not *that* Miss Wilson."

After staring at her for several moments, he reached out and reclaimed the pasteboard square. "Right there," he said, "your card states clearly that you are—"

"Harriet J. Wilson," she said as if to confirm what he read. "Harriet with only one T and without the final E. That other Miss Wilson spells her first name in the French manner. Furthermore, I have the right to the full name. She, on the other hand, purloined Wilson, merely choosing it from a hat."

The man stepped back, putting a more respectful space between them. Obviously not ready to concede his mistake, however, he said, "If you are not the courtesan, then why include that very amusing jest about having a knowledge of jewelry?"

"Jest? Sir, I see nothing humorous in the declaration, for I design and fashion jewelry. It is the manner in which I earn my living. How would you have me advertise my chosen profession?"

He said nothing for a long time. Instead, he looked from her to the tools that occupied a goodly portion of her worktable. In the silence that seemed to stretch to infinity, Harriet fancied she could hear the wheels turning inside his brain.

Finally, he made her a bow grand enough for Queen Charlotte herself. "You were in the right of it earlier, ma'am, when you said I was no gentleman. In truth, I never have been. That fact notwithstanding, I should like to think it was the blow to my head that robbed me of my ability to think coherently, and made me betray such a lack of manners to the one person whose good opinion I should have sought."

Pausing for a moment, he took a deep breath, then

let it out slowly. "Though my behavior will have given you every reason to doubt my sincerity, I beg you to believe that I am most grateful for your kindness to me this evening."

While Harriet waved aside his offer of gratitude, he turned to reclaim the ebony cane from where he had placed it on the table. When he spoke again, his voice, though formal, contained a hint of chagrin. "Madam, I fear I am long out of the habit of making apologies. For that reason, and because I have been enough of a boor for one evening, I will not trade further upon your goodwill by asking your pardon now.

"Instead," he added, "I will give you my assurance, on the unblemished name of the lady who has the misfortune to be my grandmother, that I will never mention this meeting, or you, to a living soul."

Having said his piece, he turned and exited the room.

Harriet did not follow him. Instead, she remained beside the worktable until she heard the scrape of the bolt being slid back, then the soft click of the entry door being shut behind him.

Hurrying to the vestibule, she shot the bolt home once again. Within seconds, she heard a shrill whistle, followed by the metallic clink of horseshoes on the cobblestone street just outside her door. "Where to?" she heard the jarvey ask.

"Mayfair."

"Mayfair it is, Guv."

For a long time, Harriet leaned against the door, listening to the rattle of wheels as the hackney carriage faded into the distance. When nothing remained but silence, she whispered, "Good-bye, whoever you are."

The words spoken, she pressed her fingers to her lips, as if hoping the stranger's kiss still lingered there. To her disappointment, the kiss, like the man who had given it to her, had vanished. It was as if neither had truly existed, but were mere figments of what she had always considered a totally unromantic imagination.

Much later, when she sat once again before her bedchamber window, unable to sleep, Harriet's thoughts returned to the tall, handsome stranger with the teasing gray eyes and Satan's own smile. "Papa," she whispered, talking to her father as she had done every night during the two years since his untimely death, "you warned me to stay away from men who possess the charm of the Evil One himself. Unfortunately, you neglected to tell me how, if I should meet such a person, I was to keep my foolish heart from beating against my chest like some captured wild thing."

Leaning her overheated forehead against the coolness of the windowpane, she looked toward the sky that was already showing streaks of pink. "And more importantly, Papa, you forgot to tell me how I was to erase from my thoughts the memory of that man and his soul-stealing kiss."

Chapter Two

"That'll be two and six, miss," the jarvey said.

Harriet handed the money to the driver. Then, as the hackney rattled off down the street in search of another fare, she hurried toward her own doorstep, where her cousin, Miles Gwynn, was being shaken within an inch of his life by a portly, middle-aged man in a puce coat and tan inexpressibles.

"Sir!" she said, "unhand that boy this instant."

The man, surprised by the vehemence of the order, let go of Miles, who fell to the pavement, then quickly gained his feet and scurried up the three stairs leading to the entry door. "Madam," the man said, "are you the mother of that demmed jacka-napes?"

"His mother!"

That was just what she needed, today of all days, to be asked if she were the mother of a lad who had already celebrated his tenth birthday. "I am his cousin, sir, and I will thank you to keep a civil tongue in your head when addressing me."

Harriet was in no mood for this, not after having spent the entire morning quarreling with the world's most stubborn gem supplier. Angry at having to fight

the same battle again and again, she had hoped to
return home to something resembling peace and
quiet. She wanted a cup of tea and a light repast;
after which, she had meant to lock herself in her
workroom for however many hours, days, or weeks
it took to regain her composure.

Now, here she was, faced with another angry
neighbor. "Miles," she said, "go inside and wait for
me."

The lad attempted to do her bidding, but the portly
man stopped him by grabbing the hem of his nan-
keen coat. "No, you don't," he said, giving the coat
a yank that forced Miles down the topmost step.
"You don't get off that easily, you young thatch gal-
lows. I mean to call for a constable."

Whatever prank Miles had been up to this time—
and there was never any knowing what that might
be—it certainly did not warrant the calling in of the
authorities. "Sir," Harriet said, trying for a calm she
did not feel, "can you remember what it was like to
be a young boy? Surely you got up to just such mischief when you were young . . . which, I daresay, cannot have been so very long ago." Since she pinned on
her most winning smile, she hoped the blatant flattery
would carry the day. It failed miserably.

"Madam, that boy needs to learn he cannot be en-
dangering the lives of respectable businessmen. And
I am just the man to see he is taught that lesson."

Harriet was wondering what on earth she could
do to turn the man's anger when the entry door
opened and Miles's sister stepped out into the early
afternoon sunlight. "Cousin Harriet," Anna said,
smiling sweetly, "is something amiss? Has my little
brother been playing his tricks again?"

Anna Gwynn, a willowy seventeen-year-old with
silvery blond hair and eyes the soft blue of a Siamese
kitten, had a stupefying effect upon men of all ages,

and the portly gentleman was no exception. "My dear young lady," he said, doffing his tan beaver and making her a bow so low it caused the stays in his corset to creak, "I was merely explaining to this other, er, lady, that the lad should be chastised. Though not too severely, of course. It never does to deal too harshly with the very young."

The smile Anna bestowed upon the old fool was so sweet it put Harriet in mind of a sponge cake dripping with treacle. "Oh, sir," Anna said, "I quite agree. What man with a heart in his bosom could wish to do serious harm to a young boy?"

Since the old roué had spent the past few seconds blatantly ogling Anna's very pretty bosom, he had the grace to lower his gaze.

"Allow me," she continued, "to thank you, sir, for your understanding."

"My pleasure, my dear young lady, I assure you."

While he beamed his approval upon Anna, she pushed her brother none too gently through the open door, instructing him to go immediately to his room. "And when Father comes home," she added, "I mean to tell him of this afternoon's work. If I know anything of the matter, a good caning is in your future."

"Oh, no," Miles wailed. Standing just inside the vestibule, he rubbed his rather grubby fists over his eyes as if to rid them of sudden tears. "Please, Sister, not another caning."

Since Miles's father had gone to his heavenly reward nearly a year ago, there was no fear of any such reprisals.

In the meantime, Harriet, thinking it prudent to intervene before the lad's flair for the dramatic ruined everything, joined her beautiful cousin on the steps. Taking a page from Anna's book, she shoved that young lady into the vestibule. Then, after curtsying to the astonished man, Harriet slipped in behind the chit and slammed the door.

For a full minute, the three cousins stood on the green-and-gray marble tiles, holding their collective breaths, and waited for the man to go away. After another minute passed and there was no irate banging on the door, Miles crept to the dining room window, which faced onto the street, and peeped out. "Whew!" he said. "He's gone."

"No thanks to you," his sister said, all traces of her smile vanished. "I vow, Miles, if our papa, God rest his soul, were to come through that door this very minute, I would get down on my knees and beg him to give you the whipping of your life."

"Aw, Anna, I was just having a little fun."

He turned to Harriet then. "All I did was tie a string to that old coin purse I found and drag it slowly in front of a few pedestrians. Only men, I assure you, Cousin. No ladies."

"And that is supposed to make me feel better?" Harriet asked, unmoved by his consideration for those pedestrians of the fair sex. "I vow, you are the most vexing boy. What if that dreadful man had followed through on his threat to call the constable?"

"The old puff guts," Miles said, all smiles now that the danger was passed. "You should have seen him trying to bend down enough to pick up the coin purse. I nearly split my sides laughing. What a man milliner." Turning to his sister, he said, "If he should try to call upon you, Anna, or start hanging about the corner like Charles Peckham, on the chance of an 'accidental' meeting, I hope you send him away with a flea in his ear."

"And I hope," replied his sister, her face pink with embarrassment, "that we have seen the last of your pranks."

"And heard the last of your cant conversation," Harriet added.

At this reprimand, the lad lowered his gaze to his scuffed boots. "I forgot. Your pardon, Cousin."

"Apology accepted," she said. "Now, if you please, you will go up to your room and write, legibly enough so that I can read every word, a brief yet accurate history of, oh, let me see, the reign of William and Mary of Orange."

On the instant, the boy's freckled face went from contrition to misery, putting Harriet in mind of a puppy whose beef bone has been snatched by an older dog while he was not attending. "Please, Cousin, not those two. They were so dull. Could you not just give me a caning instead?"

Since that suggestion earned him an exasperated sigh from Harriet, he ventured to make an alternate recommendation. "What say you to a paper on Richard the Third? I daresay you would find it vastly more interesting than one on their majesties. Why, just this morning I was reading all about the Battle of Bosworth Field, and—"

"Very well, you loathsome boy. Richard it is. But go now, before I change my mind and send Lucy in search of a good, strong cane."

She waited only until Miles had bounded up the stairs and was out of hearing; then she turned to his sister. "And now, miss, what is this about Charles Peckham hanging about in hopes of accidental meetings?"

Anna's cheeks turned as pale as the sprigged muslin she wore. "On my sacred honor, Cousin, I have not encouraged Mr. Peckham in any way."

Harriet did not doubt the chit's word. The trouble was, Anna was so lovely she did not *need* to encourage young men to dangle after her. Unfortunately, she had no older male relative to send the unacceptable admirers away. At least, no male relative who would trouble himself on her behalf. Her uncle Frederick, her father's younger brother, was certainly old enough, but he was a fop of the first order, interested in nothing but the figure he cut among the dandy set. Unless a person needed assistance choosing a color for a new waistcoat, Frederick Gwynn could not be counted on for help of any kind.

"Mr. Charles Peckham," Harriet continued, "is a clerk in a solicitor's office. And though in all other respects a worthy person, he will not do at all for the daughter of Sir Philip Gwynn, of Livesy Hall. Though the Hall and your father are both gone, if Sir Philip were here, he would echo what I have said, and well you know it."

"I do know it," Anna replied. "Still, Mr. Peckham has done nothing thus far but tip his hat when I walk past him. As long as he does not approach me or try to engage me in conversation, I do not know what else I can do. In all fairness, he has a right to stand on his own street."

Harriet was obliged to acknowledge the justice of that observation, but it did not totally relieve her mind. Anna could not be blamed for being beautiful, no more than she could be faulted if her numerous admirers invented ways to gain her attention. She was an intelligent girl, and she knew that she must not allow her name to be linked with those of ineligible suitors. With the family estate sold to pay her father's debts, and nothing left but the meager dowry set aside for her by her late grandfather, she must depend upon her exquisite looks and her good reputation to gain her a suitable husband.

Not for the first time, Harriet wondered what she was to do with her two charges. Anna was too lovely for her own good, and Miles was possessed of more than his fair share of boyish exuberance.

Not that he was a bad boy. All that was wrong with him was an excess of energy and no suitable outlet for it. As heir to his father's dignities, Miles should be at some respectable school, having his mind challenged by learned instructors and his body challenged by participation in daily sports.

Instead, he was cooped up in a smallish townhouse, his only companions his sister, his cousin, an ancient cook/housekeeper, and a housemaid as nearly simpleminded as made no difference. Unfortunately, at the moment there was not sufficient money for even the most modest school for the boy. However, if Harriet's jewelry business continued to progress as it had in the past six months, there would be money for school next year.

"By the way," Anna said, interrupting Harriet's unproductive worry about her cousins, "Miss Chadwick came by to pick up her brooch."

The two young ladies had made their way into the front room, which served as the reception area for clients who came to have one-of-a-kind jewelry designed for them. Anna had resumed her dusting of the glass display case, a chore that had been interrupted by the loud threats from the portly gentleman, and Harriet had settled herself into one of the two gold damask wing chairs positioned before the street-facing windows.

She still wore the russet linen gloves that perfectly matched the russet-dyed grebe feathers framing her green chip-straw bonnet, and she began slowly to peel off the gloves.

"I told Miss Chadwick last week that the pin would not be ready until tomorrow. As it happens, I finished it last night, but—"

"I know. I gave it to her."

Harriet paused, the glove only half removed. "You did what!"

"I . . . I gave Miss Chadwick the brooch."

Something like a lead weight settled in Harriet's stomach. "The diamond and emerald one? The one shaped like a sailboat tossed about by the waves?"

Anna nodded. "The woman had the receipt. I read

it carefully, and the writing was yours, showing the full twelve hundred pounds had been paid in advance by Lord Dunford."

Harriet took a deep breath, then let it out slowly, hoping the act would help her to remain calm. It failed miserably. "If you have any regard for me, Anna, please tell me that you took that particular pin from the safe."

Anna Gwynn's pretty lips trembled. "You know I have the . . . the highest regard for you, Cousin. Indeed, I should be the most ungrateful creature in nature if I did not, after all you have done for me and for Miles. But I would never dream of touching your safe, even if I knew the combination. Which I do not!"

Following the girl's impassioned outburst, Harriet studied the glass case Anna had been dusting, noticing particularly the black velvet-covered shelf with its understated display of one ring, one bracelet, one necklace, and one pair of earrings. There was a gaping space where a single pin had reposed only this morning.

Somehow, Harriet managed to swallow the groan that formed deep inside her throat. Lord Dunford's current mistress had come to claim her brooch, and Anna had given her the one from the display case!

"Miss Chadwick said she was obliged to leave town suddenly," Anna said, her voice noticeably unsteady, "and she wanted to take the brooch with her. After an hour had passed, and you had not returned, the woman began to pace back and forth, growing more impatient by the minute. At one point, she swore in a most unrefined manner, saying she meant to tell Lord Dunford not to patronize this establishment again."

When Harriet made no reply, Anna continued, all but stumbling over her words. "I . . . I know what a good client his lordship has been these past few months, and I knew you would not wish to offend him. So . . . So I put the brooch in one of the small leather boxes and gave it to the woman."

With that, Anna's eyes filled with tears. "I can see that I have done something wrong, Cousin, so please tell me what it is. You know I meant only to be helpful."

That was the worst of it, of course, for how could Harriet scream and yell—as she certainly wished to do—when she knew full well the chit had wanted to help.

Anna was only seventeen, but she was mature enough to realize that the year she and her brother had lived with Harriet had put a strain on their cousin's finances. Though it was true that Harriet's reputation as a designer of unique and beautiful jewelry had grown, and her clientele with it, it was also true that people expected to pay a female artist much less than they were willing to pay a man for a similar item.

By the same token, the gem dealers insisted on trying to foist upon her stones of inferior quality and cut, while reserving their finest merchandise for their male clients. It was just such a circumstance that had prompted the three-hour haggling match that morning with the gem supplier.

It was a constant uphill battle. If a female wished to establish herself in business, she had to be twice as gifted, twice as vigilant, and twice as frugal as a male. And all the time she was expected to refrain from any action or behavior that might be interpreted as unfeminine, while being ever watchful of her personal and business reputation.

Oh, yes! A spotless reputation was *de rigueur*. Especially for a female who had the same name as the town's most celebrated courtesan.

And now this!

"Please," Anna said, her voice breaking on the word, "tell me what I did wrong. You know I would cut off my arm before I would do anything to distress you."

Hoping her young cousin's words were hyperbole and not actual fact, Harriet rose from the chair and strode to her workroom, which was directly off the front room. After removing a very good watercolor seascape Anna had given her last month for her twenty-sixth birthday, Harriet opened the safe and took out a small, black velvet bag. Motioning the tearful young lady forward, she loosened the string, then dropped the contents of the bag into her open palm.

"I do not understand," Anna said softly, staring at the emeralds and diamonds that had been fashioned into a sailboat tossed about on the waves. "The brooch I gave Miss Chadwick—"

"Was a copy," Harriet said. "The design had turned out so well that I wanted something similar to show future customers."

This time, the tears did more than fill Anna's eyes, they spilled down her smooth, youthful cheeks at an ever-increasing rate. "The little boat was so beautiful, so exquisitely fashioned that I was positive the gems were real. I am so sorry. What . . . What can I do to make this right?"

Anna was clearly distressed, and though Harriet was inordinately fond of both her young cousins, at the moment she had no time to spare for consoling the remorseful girl. Uppermost in her mind was getting the copy back before Lord Dunford's light skirt realized the error and swore out a warrant for Harriet's arrest for fraud. The copy was worth fifty pounds at most—a far cry from the twelve hundred she had already received in payment. Received and spent.

"Go to the kitchen," Harriet said. "Tell Bertha to put on her hat, for I need her to accompany me to Miss Chadwick's house. If I hurry, perhaps I can persuade the woman that it was an honest mistake and not an attempt to cheat her."

"Please," Anna begged, making an effort to swallow her sobs, "let me come with you. After all, it was I who gave her the copy."

"No. It must be Bertha. It would not do for either of us to be seen entering that woman's house."

Following that rather pompous remark, Harriet had the grace to blush. Miss Chadwick may have accepted a piece of jewelry worth twelve-hundred pounds from a known rake and libertine, but Harriet was in no position to be pointing a self-righteous finger. Not now. After all, she had known full well the reputation of the man from whom the money came, and she had not given so much as a moment's thought to refusing the commission!

The draft for the jewelry had been written on Lord Dunford's bank; furthermore, it was not the first commission from his lordship that had come in Harriet's way in the past six months. Nor was Miss Chadwick the first recipient of the gentleman's largesse. Naturally, Harriet had been more than happy to have the repeat business, as much for the confirmation of her talent as for the money she earned.

She had never met the new Baron Dunford personally. Even though she had designed several rather expensive pieces for him, those items had been ordered by letter and picked up by his valet. For Harriet, Lord Dunford was merely a signature on a bank draft.

She had been justly proud of the items she had fashioned for his lordship, among them a gold cravat pin containing a black pearl, a pretty enamel snuffbox, and a gold fob in the shape of a peregrine falcon perched on a branch. The falcon was especially nice, as she had given him polished amber eyes, then introduced a bit of copper to the gold to duplicate the bird's pale russet breast.

She had never heard how Lord Dunford liked the jewelry. Not that she had expected to. Though in all honesty, if he had sent her a brief note, expressing his appreciation for the craftsmanship, she would not have been displeased. In fact, her curiosity had prompted her once or twice to steal a glimpse at a gentleman's cravat, in hopes of spying the black pearl pin and the man who had ordered it.

Not that she wanted to meet Lord Dunford. She merely wanted to put a face with the name. His reputation as a gambler and a libertine had reached even her ears, and each new jewelry order from him confirmed her suspicion that the gentleman's main goal in life was to "outexcess" the *ton*, where excess appeared to be the motto of the new century.

According to Harriet's records, Miss Chadwick's rented townhouse was situated no more than two blocks from Harriet's own home, close enough that she and Bertha walked the distance. Unfortunately, when they arrived, the mobcapped young housemaid who answered the door informed them that Miss Chadwick had left more than an hour ago.

"Where'd she go?" Bertha asked.

The girl's eyes grew round as saucers. "La, ma'am, the mistress don't tell me nothing. Truly she don't. All's I know is she had me pack only her newest gowns and bonnets. Filled two trunks, they did, and I don't know how many bandboxes besides."

"Never mind about her clothes," Bertha said. "Do you know when she'll return?"

The maid shook her head. "No, ma'am. Though I did hear the gentleman"—she wrinkled her nose in distaste—"that's if them Frenchies can be called gentlemen—say that most likely they wouldn't be back 'til after Michaelmas.''

Michaelmas! Harriet groaned. That was the twenty-ninth of September. Nearly six weeks away!

This could not be happening. Not to her. She was logical, rational, not some shatter-brained female with more hair than wit. Blithely ignoring the theological warnings against the sin of pride, she had always prided herself on her common sense, and on the fact that she always planned ahead, never allowing herself to be caught unprepared. Was this her punishment, then, for refusing to heed the vicar's sermon about pride going before a fall?

"By Michaelmas," Harriet said, once the maid had shut the door and Bertha had returned to her side, "I might well be in Newgate Prison."

"Oh, miss, never say so." Worry caused creases in the housekeeper's usually smiling face. "Surely there's sommit we can do."

For a moment, Harriet could not think what that might be. In the two yeas since her father's death, she had faced any number of difficult decisions, but none so frightening as the prospect of being accused of fraud. Even if she was able to explain the situation to everyone's satisfaction, the damage would be done. Her reputation would be ruined. There were always those people who embraced the belief that where there was smoke, there must be fire.

Who would trust a jeweler whose honesty had been impugned?

With the real brooch all but burning a hole in the bottom of her reticule, she knew she had but one more chance to save herself from ruin. "Come," she said, "we need a hackney."

"A hackney? Whatever for, miss?"

"We are going to Mayfair. To the home of Lord Dunford."

"Miss Harriet! You can't mean to go to that man's house!"

"I have no choice. The longer the jewelry is in my possession, the more guilty I appear. Besides, it was Lord Dunford who paid for the brooch. The *real* brooch."

"Not but what he can afford it, think on. From what them as claim to know the story be saying, his lordship won a small fortune off Lord Beasley just t'other evening."

"For all it concerns me, he may have won a dozen such fortunes. Still, Lord Dunford is the properest person to see that the jewelry he paid for reaches Miss Chadwick."

"Proper me eye! B'aint nothing proper about him! Why, he's known all over Lunnon as 'Lord Care-For-Naught.' Got respect for nothing or nobody."

"If he were Satan himself, I would still have to go to him."

"But, Miss Harriet, surely there be some other—"

"I must put the brooch in Lord Dunford's hand. Anything less, and I risk the reputation I have worked so hard to build. Now, please, Bertha, let us say no more on the subject."

Their argument at an end, Harriet hailed a passing hackney. While they climbed aboard the carriage, she crossed her fingers, and though the childish act had never before proven effective, she hoped this might be the exception. After all, she needed only a little bit of luck. Just enough to allow her to hand over the pin to his lordship, then be on her way.

Was that asking too much?

For the next half hour, as the hackney traveled toward Mayfair, that question hung in the air, a sort of modern-day sword of Damocles. How much was too much? Especially when one's livelihood hung in the balance?

London traffic was as busy as ever, and with Harriet nervous about her coming meeting with Lord Dunford, the shouting of the street vendors with their carts and barrows, as well as the noise of the horses' hooves pounding the cobbled streets, seemed to press in on her. While the jarvey maneuvered the hackney past the slower drays and wagons, to merge with the faster-moving carriages of the businessmen traveling to and from the city and gentlemen out for an afternoon's drive, his younger passenger planned what she would say to his lordship.

In actual miles, the drive from Marylebone to Mayfair was not all that far. By society's measure, however, the distance was incalculable. True, the townhouses of Mayfair were made of brick or codestone, just as those of Marylebone, with three or four stairs leading to the entrance doors and smaller, more compact stairs leading down to the servant and kitchen entries. But there the similarities ended.

Once the hackney had crossed Oxford Street and was headed toward Grosvenor Square, the residences were larger and noticeably more costly, with far more attention paid to the trim and details of the windows and doors. As well, in each square there were lovely parks with gated, wrought-iron fences meant to keep out anyone who did not truly belong.

When the driver halted the unimpressive old horse outside a handsome townhouse that would have held Harriet's own home twice over, she took a deep breath then squared her shoulders. "Wait here," she told the man.

"You wait as well," Bertha said, her tone saying that this time she would brook no argument. "And mind you keep out of sight. Your lady mother would haunt me from her grave if I was to let you go knocking at that scoundrel's door."

Without allowing Harriet a voice in the decision,

the housekeeper climbed down to the pavement and approached the thick mahogany door. When her knock was answered by a liveried footman whose haughty expression proclaimed him as a butler-in-waiting, Bertha lifted her nose in the air, giving the fellow snub for snub. Not content with the face-off, she bid the young man tell Lord Dunford that a *lady* had sommit to give him. "Ask your master if he'll be so good as to step out to the carriage for a moment."

The tall servant's eyebrows lifted and his jaw fell open. Whether this change in his expression stemmed from the fact that a woman in a hackney had called on his master, or from the shocking request he had been asked to deliver, Harriet could not tell. Whatever the reason, he shook his head. "Can't do it," he said.

At his refusal, Bertha bristled like a mastiff whose master had been threatened. "And why not, I'd like to know?"

Unbending at last, the fellow said, "On account of his lordship b'aint here."

More disappointed than she had thought possible, Harriet held her arm out the carriage window and motioned for the footman to come to her. Since she held a shilling in her gloved hand as inducement, the fellow lost no time in hurrying to the carriage, leaving Bertha standing beside the entrance door.

"Be so good as to give Lord Dunford my card," Harriet said, "and ask him if he will call on me without delay. My business with him is of the utmost urgency, and it cannot wait."

The servant took the card and the shilling, touching his forelock in respect. "Be happy to give him the card, miss, when he returns. Though when that might be, I don't rightly know, him being gone into Leicestershire for at least a fortnight."

"Leicestershire!" Harriet's despair must have sounded in her voice, for the footman hurried to inform her that his lordship had gone up to his hunting box near Kipworth on family matters. "Sommit to do with his brother, Mr. Burton Dunford."

If Harriet was surprised to discover that Lord Care-For-Naught had family feelings, she was wise enough to keep her opinions to herself. Instead, she thanked the servant, gave him an extra shilling, then waited for Bertha to rejoin her.

Convinced the fates were having a good laugh at her expense, Harriet began to formulate a new plan. There was really only one thing left for her to do, and she knew it. It remained only for her to discover if she had the courage needed. Of one thing she was certain, if she sat at home, waiting behind closed shutters to see who stormed her door first, an angry Lord Dunford or a constable with a warrant for her arrest, she would go insane.

Only when the hackney neared Marylebone did she give voice to her plan. "I have been giving it some thought, Bertha, and I believe I will take Anna and Miles on a holiday."

"A holiday? Now there's a good idea, miss."

Pleased she was to be spared another argument, Harriet breathed a sigh of relief. "I thought so. For one reason, Miles needs some country space to run about in. Room enough to allow him to wear away some of that boyish energy that gets him into mischief. For another, I should like to get Anna away from that moonling, Mr. Charles Peckham."

"If you'll listen to the wisdom of an older head, Miss Harriet, you'll go for yourself as well. You've not had a holiday since before your sainted mother took sick, and you deserve a bit of a rest. Mayhap it'll put the roses back in your cheeks."

"Do I look so drawn, then, Bertha?"

"You do and all," replied Job's comforter. "And you're much too thin. Why, in the past six months you've lost half a stone. And it's no wonder, hard as you work! And don't think I don't know why you do it. I've eyes in me head, and I know how hard it's been to pay the bills since Miss Anna and Master Miles come to live with you. And not so much as tuppence from that uncle of theirs to help with the costs."

This being a familiar topic, Harriet scarcely listened while the cook expounded on Mr. Frederick Gwynn's shortcomings, principally his devotion to his own waistcoats, and his total lack of concern for his wards. "Dumps them on you without so much as a by-your-leave. Then off he goes, never giving them another thought. I ask you, Miss Harriet, does he believe they live on air? If so, then all I can say is he never saw Master Miles put away the victuals."

"Now, Bertha. Anna and Miles are the children of my mother's sister, and my only remaining relatives. Would you have me turn my back on them?"

"No, miss, but I'm not blind, and I know the money left you by your dear father don't stretch far enough to keep a roof over the five of us."

"The very reason," Harriet said softly, "that I must not lose my good name as a jeweler."

Bertha was silent for a moment; then, as if the matter was settled, she said, "Where will you go, miss? Bath and Tunbridge Wells be best, think on, or even Brighton, but the cost of them places is dear."

The cost had been weighing heavily on Harriet's mind as well, but there were some expenses that could not be helped. They would just have to practice economy wherever possible. "We will visit Bosworth Field," she said. "Miles has been studying the Wars of the Roses in his history lessons, and I am persuaded he will adore being at the site of the great battle."

"Oh, well, if there be a battle site, then you've to say no more. The lad will be in Alt, most like."

"So I thought."

"I'm a bit rusty on history myself, miss. Where is that field you're talking about?"

"Bosworth?" Harriet replied oh so nonchalantly, hoping Bertha had not heard what the footman told her about his lordship's trip to his hunting box. "It is in Leicestershire. Not far from a little village called Kipworth."

Chapter Three

Rand stared out the window as the chaise and four continued northward, watching the great, grassy plains of the midlands speed past. Here and there the green expanse was broken by low hills and ridges, but by and large the scenery was that of patchwork fields and meadows bordered by tall hedges, stone fences, or rows of trees.

He knew the moment the carriage entered Leicester, and the realization made him sit up straight, all his senses alert. There was little flat land to speak of, and the hills, though numerous, were not very high. Still, it was the constant ups and downs of the landscape that made it perfect hunting country.

Riding to hounds, the sport of the privileged few, had been his father's favorite pastime. A member of the Quorn, James Dunford had liked nothing better than the weeks between October and Christmas—weeks he spent at his hunting box, in the company of his sports-mad cronies. Because his father loved the place, Rand had learned to detest it.

He detested it still.

Like almost everything else that had once belonged to James Dunford, the hunting box had been part of the entail and had passed down to the heir, the new Baron Dunford. It was all Rand's now. The box, as well as Ford Park, two lesser estates, and a yearly income in excess of ten thousand pounds were all his. Yet he took no pleasure in any of it.

For perhaps half an hour, the chaise continued on the busy Holyhead Road; then it took the less traveled country road that finally passed through the little village of Kipworth. It was a pretty place, owing much of its charm to the irregular rooflines and frontages of the gingerbread-colored shops and cottages. As well, the green was unusually spacious, with a mixture of black-faced and gray-faced sheep grazing as peacefully as their ancestors had done decades earlier.

Two miles beyond the village, a country lane gave access to the crushed-stone carriageway that led to the hunting box.

Even before they reached the house, Rand heard the excited yelping of the hounds in the kennels. The familiar sound caused a tightening in his chest, an unexpected rush of emotion. It had been more than a dozen years since he had set foot on the place, yet it looked and sounded much the same. It even smelled the same, a fact that awakened memories he did not wish revived. Memories of that last, painful encounter with his father.

The house itself, a rectangle fashioned of mellowed tan brick, was unpretentious in its architecture, and rather small, containing no more than a dozen bedrooms, some of them quite cramped and austere. Not that any of his father's many visitors had cared a fig for their accommodations. For the true sportsman, nothing mattered but the stables, and that brick building, which stood perhaps two hundred yards to the far right of the carriageway, was magnificent. Nearly twice the size of the house, the stables were no more than twenty years old, and their design and construction had been James Dunford's pride and joy.

Not his sons. His stables!

Rand had not meant to return to Kipworth. Not ever. No more than he meant ever to take up residence at Ford Park, in West Sussex, the primary seat of the five previous Barons Dunford. So far, he had managed to avoid his ancestral home; unfortunately, he could not ignore the plea of his grandmother, the dowager Lady Dunford. In the letter he had received from that imperious lady, she had written that his brother had walked away from Oxford and was holed up in the hunting box.

"I do not, of course, have the entire story. What little I know was relayed to me by a friend, who heard it from her son, who is also at Oxford. According to my informant, Burton has become enamored of a totally unsuitable female. 'Besotted with a tavern keeper's daughter,' were my friend's exact words. And from Burton's actions, it would appear the romance did not progress as he had hoped."

As if unable to contain her displeasure a moment longer, the dowager added, "Love! Bah! What folly! And what idiots that emotion makes of men, young and old alike."

Since she had followed those pithy remarks with several quite unladylike epithets that gave further evidence of her disgust of the subject so beloved of the poets, it was obvious to Rand that she considered Burton Dunford's present despair the result of nothing more than a case of foolish calf-love.

In this belief, however, she was mistaken.

"What I wish you to do," her ladyship had continued, "is to go to Kipworth and see that this despondency does not lead your brother into doing something even more foolish. At his age, a failed love affair can seem like the end of the world, and I should hate to think that he might be taking it so badly that it would lead him to do himself an injury."

Somehow, his brother did not strike Rand as the sort who would die for love. Still, their grandmother feared something of the sort, and her acquaintance with Burton far surpassed his.

"Make the boy understand that a broken heart is not the end of the world. Explain to him that there are hundreds, nay, thousands of beautiful girls yet to be met. In the past few months, Randolph, I have often wondered if your brains were to let, but if there is one subject you know to a fare-thee-well, that subject is beautiful lady birds. Give Burton the benefit of your experience."

His grandmother had ended her unflattering remarks by stating her dependence on Rand's loyalty, if not to his name, then to her. Confronted by what was clearly emotional blackmail, what was he to do but placate the elderly lady? After all, she was the only person in the world he cared tuppence about. She was the only person who had stood by him twelve years ago when the scandal broke. Everyone else—his father, his mother, even Burton, who had always followed Rand about, adoration and hero worship in every glance—had turned their backs on him, believing every word that spewed from that lying wench's mouth.

As usual, thoughts of Belle Coombs and her devious, money-grubbing father left a bitter taste in Rand's mouth. True, his own father, a coldhearted tyrant who had no use for any creature—dog, horse, or human—who did not live up to his rigid standards, had never had much use for his oldest son. Still, to whip his heir senseless, then send him to Barbados in disgrace, without allowing him even a word in his own defense, had been unforgivable.

Rand had been in his second year at Oxford. Just turned eighteen, he had been a year younger than Burton was now. Naturally, he had thought himself a downy fellow, bang-up to the mark, as the saying went. It took less than a fortnight of laboring in the cane fields outside Bridgetown, to cure him of that bit of self-deception.

Bridgetown, Barbados. The very words set his anger at the boil!

Anger. Hate. Loathing. These were his principal memories. He had hated the islands. He hated them still: the swaying palms, the white-sand beaches, the clear blue waters of the Atlantic, and the never-ending sunshine. Let others call the Caribbean paradise; to Rand it was hell on earth. In addition, that particular section of Hades was filled with the dregs of humanity: drunken sailors, pirates, slave traders, Europeans who had fled their homelands, leaving those who remained to the tender mercies of Napoleon's army, and Englishmen who had disgraced their families and were, like Rand, pariahs no longer acceptable in polite society.

The first few months, all that had saved his sanity was his nightly fantasy of returning to England and proving to one and all that he was not a person to be condemned on the word of a felon and his slatternly daughter. Naturally, those were the dreams of a naive boy, and he put them away soon enough. Cruelly hard work, and even crueler men—men who thought nothing of beating a green lad half to death and stealing what little money he possessed—had a maturing effect upon Rand, forcing him to grow up fast.

As he grew, the opinions of others had come to mean less and less to him, until one day he had awakened and realized that he cared not one whit what anyone thought of him. To hell with the lot of them!

His one remaining goal was to get his hands on enough money to buy return passage to England.

And the means by which he obtained that money were far less important to him than the outcome. His one wish, to face James Dunford and to hear him beg for his son's forgiveness.

Lady Luck, though a notoriously fickle mistress, had finally smiled upon Rand by putting him in company with a pompous Frenchman who fancied himself an expert at whist. At least ten years Rand's senior, Antoine de la Croix, a slave trader only just returned from delivering his wretched human cargo to one of the large plantations outside Bridgetown, had staggered into Pepe's grog shop late one evening.

The shop, which served the needs of the poorer islanders, was little more than a thatched roof, a dirt floor, a bar, and a few rickety tables. Rand sat at one of those tables, playing small-stakes whist with a trio of local men who toiled alongside him in the cane fields. It was payday, and he had already won most of the other men's pitiful wages.

The tall, dark-eyed de la Croix, spying a European with a small stack of coins in front of him, had smiled, putting Rand in mind of a fox that had just discovered the door to the poultry house standing open. Drawing a pistol that was strapped to his thigh, he used the rounded metal butt cap to hit one of the islanders in the head and knock him to the ground, which was covered by at least a week's worth of spilled food, rum, and tobacco spittle. After firing both shots into the air, and sending the three islanders scurrying away like vermin from a doomed ship, de la Croix took the now empty chair opposite Rand, opened a small leather pouch, and spilled several gold coins onto the table.

"Try your luck with a real gambler," the Frenchman said, his words so slurred it was obvious he had already had more than one pull off a bottle of rum.

"With pleasure," Rand said, gathering up the cards and beginning to shuffle.

He was as sober as a judge, for he was unwilling to spend so much as a groat of his hard-earned money on the island's fermented cane liquor. And yet, it did not bother his conscience in the least that de la Croix was already three parts disguised, or that he immediately called for another bottle. All that mattered was that the man's pockets were filled with gold—gold Rand would gladly add to his savings. If the slaver was fool enough to try his luck while too castaway to know what he was doing, let it be on his head.

In less than two hours, the contents of the leather pouch were stacked before Rand. Every last coin. He had shown the arrogant de la Croix the error of his ways, and in doing so he had gained the means to leave Barbados forever. "Thank you," he said. Placing the deck of cards on the table, he reached for the coins. "It has been a pleasure."

All might have been well if the Frenchman had taken his losses like a gentleman. Instead, he caught Rand's wrist, attempting to stop him from raking the coins into his hat. "Oh, no you don't," he bellowed. "That is my money."

"It *was* your money," Rand said quietly, staring coldly at the man's hand on his wrist. "Now it is mine."

"You cheated," the Frenchman bellowed. "You fuzzed the cards!"

Furious at the accusation, Rand dealt the man a facer, knocking him to the filth-strewn floor.

After righting himself with difficulty, the Frenchman wiped his befouled hands on his britches, then drew a dirk from inside his coat. "For this insult, *monsieur*, you will pay with your life! No one knocks Antoine de la Croix to the ground and lives to see another sunrise."

The steel of the long, straight-bladed dagger bore traces of some poor wretch's blood, and Rand was not so foolish as to dismiss the present threat to his own health. "I think not," he said, pulling a knife of his own. At last he had enough money to buy passage home, and he was not about to be cheated out of it. Neither the money nor his life.

The Frenchman, his dark eyes filled with hate, looked toward the bar, where a burly fellow stood with his arm around one of the serving wenches, bargaining with her for half an hour of her time. "Pierre!" de la Croix yelled. "Hold this jackal while I teach him some manners."

The fellow came forward eagerly enough, obviously as willing to fight as he was to wench. Unfortunately, he had misjudged his man, for Rand waited only until Pierre was within arm's reach; then he grabbed the empty rum bottle from the table, swung quickly, and hit the burly fellow squarely in the forehead. Pierre dropped like a newly axed tree.

De la Croix, staring at his fallen henchman, did not move forward or attempt to trade blows with Rand. Without the aid of his accomplice, he was afraid to confront a man armed as well as he. "I will not forget this," he said, backing away from Rand. "It is a small island, *monsieur*, and I will find you. And when next we meet, you have my word on it, I will cut out your heart and feed it to the sharks."

Rand did not doubt him for a minute. And for that reason, he did not return to the grass hut he had shared with five other workmen for the past dozen years. Considering his meager possessions well lost, he went directly to the docks and booked passage on a boat leaving Bridgetown the next morning, thereby robbing de la Croix of his revenge.

As for Rand's own, long-dreamed-of revenge, it was not to be. As luck would have it, by the time he arrived on England's damp, foggy shores, his father had been lain to rest beside his mother, in the church-yard at Latchmere, in West Sussex.

The man who had figured as his nemesis for almost a dozen years was gone, and with James Dunford's demise, his son had no target for his anger. Refusing to take his place as lord and master of Ford Park was a minor rebellion, but it was the only rebellion left to him. That, and doing everything within his power to ruin the name that had once meant everything to his father.

Now, here Rand was at the hunting box, answering his grandmother's call for help. As though Burton would listen to anything his older brother had to say. It was not as if he were Burton's guardian, or had any control whatever over the boy. Their father had seen to that by appointing a pair of solicitors to handle his younger son's finances and to see to his education.

Rand was not his brother's keeper. They were not even friends. And if their one and only meeting since his return to England was anything to go by, Burton wanted nothing to do with him. As for giving his brother unsolicited advice on the subject of his love life, Rand could just imagine how well the young man would welcome that.

He could, however, protect the young fool from harm. Not self-inflicted injury, as the dowager feared, but from the revenge promised him by the three older brothers of the tavern keeper's daughter.

Not willing to trust the validity of the story as told by his grandmother's informant, Rand had gone to Oxford and asked a few questions of his own. That was how he had found out about the three Wexham brothers and their threats.

According to his brother's best friend, Burton had heard rumors that the girl he loved, Flo Wexham, was seeing someone else as well as him. At first he refused to believe the rumors, but upon spying the lovers in an embrace, he had been obliged to admit that he was being played for a fool.

Hurt and disillusioned, Burton had told Flo he never wanted to see her again, a circumstance that led her to elope with another of her lovers, the blacksmith's son. Unfortunately, the girl's three older brothers considered Burton's retreat in the light of a breach of contract; so one evening the Wexhams waylaid him and threatened to beat him senseless if he did not supply their sister with a dowry of one hundred quid, payable to them.

Obviously Burton did not have the money—either that or he had refused to pay as a matter of principle. Whatever his reasons, he had fled from the threatened wrath of the trio, and had gone to ground like a wounded fox, choosing to hide out in the hunting box.

Now, here Rand was as well, and for all he knew, his brother would greet his arrival with no more pleasure than he would that of the Wexhams. He was still wondering how his and Burton's second meeting would go when the coachman reined in the job horses only a few feet from the shallow overhang at the entrance of the hunting box. Before his valet could jump down from his place beside the coachman and offer his assistance to the passenger, the heavy walnut door was flung open and a gnomelike little man in a smock and leather breeches hurried toward the coach.

"Master Rand," the wizened old fellow said, his broad smile revealing numerous gaps where teeth were missing, "be it really ye?"

"Eli, you old relic!"

Rand leaped to the ground and caught the old huntsman's hand between both of his, giving it a squeeze of genuine pleasure. "I never expected to see you again, Eli, not this side of Hades in any event. I thought surely you would have been planted in the churchyard years ago."

"They give it a try once or twice," he said, his wink contorting his already homely face, "but seems I b'aint handsome enough for heaven, nor ugly enough for hell."

For as long as Rand could remember, Eli Porter had been huntsman here, the man responsible for the routine of the kennel and the breeding, care, and training of the hounds. When Rand was still a very young boy, he used to measure his yearly growth by comparing his own height to that of the little man. Now, of course, Rand was more than six feet tall, and he towered over Eli's diminutive four feet.

If memory served, however, no one measured up to Eli Porter when it came to simple goodness of heart. In that area, Eli was a giant.

"It is a pleasure to see you again."

"Thankee, sir. I'm that glad ye've come home at last, Master Rand. *Yer lordship*, I should say. It be time and then some for ye to take yer rightful place as head of the Dunfords. And a fine master ye'll make, I be thinking."

"In that opinion," said a petulant voice from just inside the doorway, "I fear you stand alone."

"Burton," Rand said, looking at the slender young man whose dark blond hair and gray eyes were so like his own. "So you are here."

"An astute observation," the younger man replied, his words only slightly slurred. "Were you always so quick to grasp the obvious?"

Telling himself he would gain nothing by giving vent to his temper, Rand merely smiled. "You would be wise, you silly cawker, to hold your tongue. Otherwise, I might be tempted to call for a bucket of cold water so I can dunk your head in it. A good dousing would probably do you a world of good. If nothing else, it would rid you of that surly expression. It might even sober you up a bit."

"I am quite sober."

"Of course you are. How foolish of me to have jumped to such a conclusion. Especially when I have nothing to base it on save the rather sorry state of your clothing, your slurred speech, and the foul aroma of stale home brew that hangs about your person like an aura."

Unless Rand's nose was playing him false, his brother had passed the entire fortnight since leaving the university by attempting to drown his sorrows. "One wonders as well, Burton, about that other, shall we say less-than-appealing aroma. The one emanating from your clothing."

At Burton's age, his beard was still light. Even so, a scraggly growth adorned his chin and jawline, giving him an unkempt look. "In addition to wanting a shave and a bath, you are in dire need of a change of clothes, for unless I miss my guess, you have been casting up your accounts."

Burton's hands balled into fists. "All I need," he said, "is for you to go away and leave me alone. Better yet, do the world a favor and go to hell!"

Eli gasped, but Rand did not so much as bat an eye. "Very likely I shall go there eventually, but not from anything I have said to you."

Rand sighed. He had traveled more than a hundred miles, and he was in no mood to play dogsbody to a drunken youth. Getting right to the purpose of his visit, he said, "As I understand the situation, Burton, you have taken an early holiday from the university, and all because of a female with a preference for blacksmiths."

His brother drew himself up to his full height, which was slightly less than six feet, attempting a hauteur that sat ill on the shoulders of an inebriated nineteen-year-old. "How dare you meddle in things that do not concern you? What I have or have not done is none of your affair, sir, and I will thank you not to mention the subject again."

"I would like nothing better, I assure you. Unfortunately, our grandmother is concerned for your well-being. It was her wish that I come here to see if I could talk some sense into you."

"The devil, you say!" Burton's face turned red with anger. "How could Grandmother believe I would take advice from you? From you, of all people! If the idea were not so insulting, I vow I would be laughing my head off."

"Have a care," Rand said, his voice ominously low. "Do not try my patience too far."

"I try *your* patience! What hypocrisy! I may have acted the fool by giving my heart unwisely, but my sins are nothing to yours. I truly loved Flo."

Softening slightly, Rand said, "You will love again, I assure you."

"Never!"

Rand knew better than to waste his breath trying to convince his brother that there were other fish in the sea. Instead, he said, "Never is a long time, you silly mooncalf."

Taking exception to the name-calling, Burton said, "A mooncalf I may be, but at least I did not disgrace the family by leaving the girl with my by-blow swelling her belly. What a pity you cannot say the same!"

Chapter Four

After traveling for two days, Harriet was more than happy to climb down from the hired coach that had brought them to Kipworth, Leicestershire. With turnpikes to pay every eight or ten miles, plus the cost of the post chaise, and the vails she was obliged to give when the postboy held out his hand at each change of horses, the trip had already cost more than fifteen pounds. Since she had promised Miles and Anna a full week in the country, she was happy to see that the posting inn where they were to stay was a modest one.

The main part of the inn, which had been built at least a century earlier, boasted three stories, while the later additions, which ran to the rear on both the left and the right of the original structure, were two stories each. The once red brick had faded to a soft pink, and like the outside door that led to the tap-room, the thick oak of the dutch-style entryway was black with age. Over the top half of the divided door hung a wooden sign bearing the name "the Rose and Crown." Beneath that sign was a smaller one announcing lectures and recitals held in the assembly room on the second Thursday of each month, and subscription assemblies held on the third Thursday.

According to the posting agent in London, the

Rose and Crown catered exclusively to sportsmen during the hunting season. During the off season, or so Harriet had been assured, the inn depended upon the patronage of respectable families on holiday. Even so, when the foursome from Marylebone climbed down from the coach, Harriet approached the inn with some trepidation. Having heard that some innkeepers were loath to accept ladies unaccompanied by gentlemen, she had already made up her mind what she must do.

"Good afternoon," she said, nodding to the portly man who descended the narrow stairs, wiping his hands on the front of the large apron that protected his shirt and waistcoat, "I am Miss Wilson. And you are?"

"Shimmerhorn," he said, looking from her to the postboy who was even now removing their luggage from the boot of the hired coach. "Ian Shimmerhorn. But the Rose and Crown don't take unescorted females. Best try down the high street, at the—"

"We are here for a sennight's holiday," Harriet said, pretending not to hear him, "and I require accommodation for myself, my two cousins, and our maid. If need be, Miss Gwynn and I can share a room, but Sir Miles will, of course, want a room of his own."

With more than a hint of suspicion in his eyes, the innkeeper stared at the ten-year-old who was even now offering to assist the ostler with the horses. "*Sir* Miles you say?"

Remembering the adage "In for a penny, in for a pound," Harriet replied in the affirmative. "Sir Miles Gwynn of Livesy Hall, in Middlesex." Then, with all the hauteur she could manage, she added, "I trust you can furnish us with a private dining room. Naturally, I cannot allow Sir Miles and his sister to dine in the company of strangers."

Since the invoking of her cousin's title had not produced the awe-inspiring effect Harriet had hoped for, it was as well for their immediate future that Anna chose that moment to enter the inn. The young lady had removed her chip-straw bonnet and was holding it by the strings, and as she paused in the doorway, the afternoon sun turned to silver the blond curls that framed her exquisite face.

"Cousin," she said, her cornflower blue eyes alight with pleasure, "how fortunate that we stopped at this particular inn, for the ostler says there is a litter of kittens in the stable, and the dear creatures are only three days old." Turning the full force of her sweet smile upon the innkeeper, she said, "May my brother and I go see them, sir?"

Ian Shimmerhorn may have been approaching sixty, and his gray hair may have been thinning noticeably on top, but he was no more immune than any other male to the smile of a beautiful young lady. "Kittens?" he muttered, much as if the word had not previously come his way. Then, as though calling himself to attention, he replied, " 'Course you may see them, miss. Tim'll show you the way. Meanwhile, I'll have the boot boy take your traps up to your room."

That evening, the three cousins partook of an early dinner; then, with Lucy occupying the trundle beneath Anna's bed, they all retired to their separate rooms. Unlike their cousin, who felt the burden of responsibility for the valuable emerald brooch she carried in her reticule, Anna and Miles slept soundly and were still abed the next morning when Harriet came below stairs in search of tea and toast. She was determined to see Lord Dunford first thing, and hoping to present a businesslike picture, she had donned her nut-brown poplin traveling dress and the close-fitting York tan bonnet that matched her pelisse.

"Once I have broken my fast," she informed the innkeeper, "I should like to hire a conveyance of some kind."

"Sorry, miss, but the gig is at the smith's. Wheel broke t'other day. All's left is a donkey cart, and though the cart is reasonably sound, the donkey is old enough to have been one of the pair Noah took on the ark."

"Is the animal dependable? Is he likely to run away with me?"

Shimmerhorn shook his head. "He'll not run away. That I can promise right enough. But—"

"Then I am persuaded the cart will do well enough for my purpose, especially since I do not mean to leave the neighborhood."

Less than an hour later, Harriet climbed aboard the little two-wheeled vehicle, with its woven-cane seat, and took the reins from the young ostler.

"Lord Dunford's hunting box be two miles down t'lane," the fellow said, eyeing the shilling she held in her hand. "Just keep t'wall to yer left. Most likely ye'll hear t'hounds ayelping before ye see t'carriage-way. Any rood, ye can't miss t'place."

Hopeful of completing her mission by midmorning, Harriet had thanked the ostler, tossed him the shilling, then clicked her tongue at the donkey, giving the animal the order to be on his way. Apparently happy to be trading his musty stall for a walk in the sunshine, the little donkey complied, and for a time everything went smoothly.

As promised, the low stone wall was easy enough to follow, but within half a mile, Harriet began to have her doubts about ever reaching her destination. The little donkey was the oldest creature she had ever seen, and though he plodded along the dusty lane without complaint, neither needing nor heeding direction from her, Harriet was certain she could have made better time on foot.

Not that walking was an alternative. If she did not arrive at the hunting box in some sort of equipage, no matter how modest, any self-respecting butler could be expected to shut the door in her face.

They had traveled no more than a mile when the donkey's long ears twitched and he brayed softly. To the right of the lane, at a break in the quickthorn hedges, grew half a dozen small apple trees, and to Harriet's dismay, the animal moved toward those trees, then came to a complete stop. Before she guessed his intention, he began to lip a stunted pippin that had fallen to the ground beneath an equally stunted tree.

"No, no," Harriet said kindly, pulling gently on the reins, "you cannot stop now. Time enough for a treat after we have seen his lordship." Clicking her tongue, she said, "Go on. There's a good donkey."

The animal paid her no heed. Instead, he caught the tiny apple with his yellowed front teeth, then raised his head and let the pippin roll back on his tongue to his molars.

"Please," she said, flicking him with the reins, "we must be on our way. I give you my word we will stop on the return journey."

His only response was to chomp down loudly on the fruit.

"Oh, bother!" Harriet said a minute later, when the beast seemed in no hurry to leave. "Do get on with it, old fellow. I do not have all day."

Apparently, the little donkey had no such time constraints, for when he finished eating the first pippin, he nudged at the leaves of a low-hanging branch until he spied another likely specimen. Pleased with his discovery, he pulled the fruit from the branch and resumed his repast.

"Oh, no!" Harriet said, yanking on the reins. "Enough is enough. Now move!"

It was no use. No matter how much she prompted, cajoled, or threatened, the donkey merely stood there chomping, for all the world as if the little apples had been his purpose for leaving the inn yard in the first place.

Growing exasperated, Harriet finally yelled at him. "Move, you stupid old fool!" She might as well have saved her breath.

Wondering what she had done to deserve this vexation, she decided to climb down and take hold of the bridle, to see if she could pull the obstinate creature forward. The idea had no sooner entered her mind than she heard the distant pounding of hooves. Up ahead the lane curved, so she could see nothing, but from the ever-increasing sound, the horse was large, galloping at a great speed, and headed her way.

The lane was narrow, and she and the cart were on the wrong side and apparently not going anyplace soon. Realizing the potential for serious injury to herself and the animal, Harriet slapped the reins forcefully against the donkey's back. "Go!" she yelled. "Do you wish to be trampled, you stupid beast?"

His only response was another loud chomp.

With her heart pounding harder than the hooves of the oncoming horse, Harriet prayed the rider was both skilled and paying attention. For his sake as well as theirs. If she knew anything of the matter, he and the horse would be on top of her within seconds, and the result could only be disastrous.

Should she cry out a warning? Or should she remain quiet and hope for a miracle?

Not certain what was best, she glanced quickly at

the donkey to see if he had heard the noise. If he panicked and bolted at the last minute, he could easily overturn the cart, guaranteeing their mutual fate beneath the all-too-lethal hooves. Not willing to trust her luck to the placid animal, who appeared interested in nothing save the pippins, Harriet dropped the reins, yanked her skirts up above her knees, and prepared to save herself by leaping from the cart and taking her chances on the protection of the trees.

Before she could jump, however, she spied the horse. He was, indeed, large—at least sixteen hands high. A beautiful chestnut, he galloped proudly, his mane flying in the wind.

To Harriet's relief, the gentleman in the saddle saw the donkey cart while there were still several feet of lane remaining between them, and with the slightest pressing of his legs against his mount's ribs, he asked the animal to jump. In the next instant, the rider leaned forward, the chestnut's powerful muscles bunched, and as one, horse and man all but flew over the low stone wall, clearing it with ease.

Once the threat of danger was past, Harriet fell back against the cane seat, trembling like a blancmange. With her breath coming in gasps, she watched as the chestnut galloped across the undulating field. More grateful than she could say that neither the animals nor the humans had come to harm, she looked heavenward and mouthed a soundless, "Thank you."

She assumed that would be an end to the incident, but while she struggled to quiet her breathing, the rider slowed, then turned the chestnut. Apparently no worse for the unplanned jump, the horse trotted back to the wall, his neck held high and arched. Harriet's heart had not yet resumed its normal cadence when the rider reined in the animal and called out to her. "Are you all right, ma'am?"

"Perfectly," she replied. "Thanks in no small part

to your expert handling of the reins. But what of you, sir? I pray you suffered no ill effects from the sudden jump."

"None whatsoever."

"And the horse?"

The man reached down and patted the chestnut's neck. "Mercury is a hunter, and I would guess that he has jumped this very wall untold numbers of times while in pursuit of a fox."

"I am inordinately glad to hear it."

Suddenly realizing that her skirts were still above her knees, Harriet blushed profusely, then hurriedly pushed the poplin down over her limbs. When she looked up once again, the rider had dismounted and was vaulting over the wall. Only then did Harriet notice that his head was bare.

Her embarrassment doubled when she spied an expensive-looking curly brimmed beaver lying in the dust, where it had obviously fallen during the jump. While the tall gentleman bent to retrieve the chapeau, Harriet apologized for the entire mishap. "If it is of any consolation to you, sir, nothing like this will ever happen again."

"Never?" he asked, scooping up the gray beaver and using the sleeve of his steel-blue coat to brush the dirt from the brim.

"Never. For even as we speak I am planning the murder of that blasted donkey."

The man chuckled. "Have you a weapon? Or shall I lend you my saddle pistol?"

Though relieved to hear the teasing quality in his voice, Harriet declined his offer. "A bullet would be too swift, too merciful for that recalcitrant beast. Nothing will satisfy me but to strangle him with my bare hands. After all, some compensation is due me for the fright inflicted upon—"

The words died on her lips, for the gentleman had

finally looked up from the repairs to his hat, and Harriet saw his entire face for the first time. "You!" she said, recognizing the man whose wounds she had tended several months earlier. The stranger whose kiss she had never forgotten.

Her surprise was mirrored by his. "Miss Wilson!"

Chapter Five

"Sir," Harriet said, still unable to believe the testimony of his eyes, "is it really you, or have I actually been trampled beneath the hooves of that beautiful chestnut and had my brains addled?"

Rand was having serious doubts about his own mental stability. Surely this was some sort of waking dream, for how could Miss Harriet Wilson be here? In Leicestershire?

Since that night six months ago, when she had been his angel of mercy and had taken him into her home and tended his wounds, he had imagined meeting her again someday. Never in his wildest dreams, however, had he expected to encounter her here in Kipworth, of all places, not a mile from his hunting box. "Ma'am," he said, "why are you here?"

"Here?" she repeated. "Do you mean in this lane, or in Leicestershire?"

As if suddenly remembering that he had no right to question any activity of hers, he begged her pardon for his rudeness. "It is only that I am surprised to meet you again."

"Under the circumstances, sir, I should think 'amazed' a better description of my own feelings. When I set out from the Rose and Crown this morning, had I been granted a hundred guesses as to who

I would encounter, I would have used the lot and still not thought of you."

"The Rose and Crown, you say. Then you are not visiting friends in the neighborhood?"

She shook her head. "I am acquainted with no one here. Or I should say, I *thought* I knew no one. Though to tell the truth, if our meetings continue to be preceded by narrow escapes from danger, perhaps it would be prudent of us to deny the acquaintance. Who can say what fate may have planned for us on the occasion of our third meeting?"

She shuddered as if frightened at the prospect, but Rand was not deceived. "The intrepid Miss Wilson afraid? I cannot credit it. Why, had Wellington numbered among his troops only a half-dozen Miss Wilsons, Bonaparte would have been defeated years ago."

"And had poor Mr. Brummel possessed your gift for flattery, sir, that gentleman would still be the Prince Regent's favorite."

Rand laughed. She had a sharp tongue; he liked that. Especially after months of being fawned over and pursued by every young lady in London, and all because of his title and wealth. "Since the prospect of further danger has you, er, quaking with fear, Miss Wilson, I propose we not leave our third meeting in fate's hands."

"No?"

"Definitely not. If you are ready to return to the inn, what say you to my escorting you there? After we have rid ourselves of your present mode of transportation, it would give me great pleasure to show you the attractions of the village."

"And those would be?"

Rand was obliged to search his memory. After an absence of a dozen years, the only place he could remember that might possibly qualify as an attraction was the ancient church at the top of the high street. "There is St. Agnes's Church."

"A church." The dryness of her tone, plus the slight lifting of her delicately arched eyebrows told him plainly that she did not believe he had ever set foot in such a place.

Pretending not to notice her obvious skepticism, he said, "St. Agnes's is not to be missed."

"The reason being?"

She would have to ask! Unwilling to cry craven, Rand tried to recall the wording on the little plaque to the right of the thick, battered old door. "Because the structure is said to be, er . . ."

When he was obliged to fall silent, the lady chuckled. "For a moment there, sir, you very nearly fooled me into believing you possessed actual knowledge of a house of worship."

"I do. That is, I did. At one time."

" 'At one time.' Oh, of course. I should have known. 'Tis the age-old cry of those who are without proof of their professed talents: 'I *used* to know.' "

"Wait!" he said, undeterred by her lack of faith in him, "I have it now." Employing a singsong voice worthy of the most seasoned guide, he said, " 'St. Agnes's is a testimony to Norman ingenuity.' "

"You just made that up!"

"No, no. You have my word on it. I was reciting from a little plaque, one I will be happy to show you, along with Kipworth's other, er, landmarks of historical interest."

Rand might have forgotten the wonders of the little village, but one thing had remained fixed in his memory, and that was Miss Harriet Wilson's pansy eyes. Now those eyes were alight with amusement. "You would have me believe, sir, that you are an admirer of antiquities?"

He placed his hand over his heart as if her doubt distressed him. "That surprises you?"

"Admittedly. Considering the circumstances of our previous meeting, not to mention the lateness of the hour on that occasion, I had supposed your primary interests to be of a slightly more worldly nature. The times I thought of you, it was never as a man given to studious pursuits."

So, she had thought of him. Rand was pleased to hear it, but if the sudden color in her cheeks was anything to go by, she was less than pleased to have revealed that particular piece of information. Afraid if she was too embarrassed she might not allow him to be her guide, he hurried to add the only other fact that came to mind. "The walls of the church are comprised almost entirely of materials taken from the ruins of Roman buildings."

"How very interesting, to be sure. Making use of the Roman ruins would certainly qualify as Norman ingenuity. Pray, tell me more."

"And," he added, having exhausted his knowledge of the subject, "I have it on good authority that visitors—especially ladies only just up from London—find the church fascinating."

Though Rand would have sworn she was not displeased by his invitation, she declined the offer. "Though you see me positively agog at the promise of such a treat, I fear I cannot accept."

Surprised at the disappointment he felt, Rand asked her why.

"One day soon," she said, "this vexatious donkey will have eaten his fill of apples, and when that happy event occurs, I must complete the errand that brought me to Leicestershire."

"You are come on an errand? How fortunate, for I am at my best when discharging errands."

"Thank you, sir, but—"

Before she could refuse him again, he said, "Are you acquainted with the area? If not, you will find me an excellent guide. I came here often as a boy, and I know the neighborhood quite—"

He broke off his explanation, for at his offer of escort, all signs of her previous lightheartedness left her face. "I am bound for a hunting box," she said, though obviously reluctant to disclose the fact. "One belonging to Lord Dunford."

"Lord Dunford!" Taken by surprise, he blurted out, "Why in heaven's name are you going there?"

The question was beyond impertinent, and the moment it left his lips, the lady's cheeks went from pink to fiery red. Realizing that he had crossed the line at last, Rand begged her pardon. "When I dressed this morning, I must have left my manners in the clothespress."

"Think nothing of it, sir. Moments ago you saved my life, and the debt of gratitude I feel as a result of your quick thinking makes it unlikely that I would censure any behavior of yours. As it happens, I have a package to deliver to Lord Dunford."

"A package?"

"A piece of jewelry, actually."

In the past six months, Rand had ordered any number of pieces from her. Sending business her way was his only means of repaying her for rescuing him from those two cutthroats. And, of course, it helped ease his conscience about having insulted her, mistaking her for the notorious courtesan, Harriette Wilson. Still, he could recall nothing he had ordered that would necessitate her coming all the way to Kipworth to make the delivery.

"You may have forgotten, sir, that I design and fashion jewelry."

"No, I remembered that. I was just surprised that you delivered the items yourself. And at such a distance from Marylebone. Is Dunford expecting you?''

She looked down at her hands, and for a moment Rand thought she meant not to answer. When she lifted her gaze, her eyes were very serious. "His lordship knows nothing of the matter. I am come on my own behalf, in the hope of diverting a disaster."

Having twice witnessed firsthand her steadiness in the face of danger, Rand did not question the use of so dramatic a word. "If I may be of service to you in any way, Miss Wilson, you have but to ask."

In a very few sentences, she explained how the paste brooch had been mistaken for the real one. "I am sure you understand, sir, the consequences to my livelihood, and ultimately to my life, if I were accused of fraudulent practices."

Having once been as near destitute as made no difference, Rand understood the situation all too well. Just as he understood that it was Sally Chadwick's greed and impatience that had precipitated this debacle. After noticing how concern was pulling down the corners of Miss Wilson's pretty mouth, Rand experienced a desire to throttle his one-time mistress.

Not that he ever expected to see Sally again. He had ended their liaison months ago, shortly after the incident in front of Miss Wilson's townhouse. And the rumor going around town was that Sally had decided to bestow her favors upon a wealthy Frenchman—one newly arrived from Barbados.

As for her new protector, if it was Antoine de la Croix, and he had begun his plan for revenge against Rand, he was a fool. He would need to do more than tempt away an already abandoned mistress to cause Rand the least inconvenience.

"The mere hint of scandal," Miss Wilson continued, bringing Rand's thoughts back from his sworn enemy, "would put paid to my career as a jeweler. For that reason, I need not tell you how upset I was when I discovered that Miss Chadwick was no longer in town. Or why I had no choice but to come here, so I might place the real brooch in Lord Dunford's hands."

She felt she had no choice. Damnation! This was not what Rand had had in mind. He had wanted to help her, to make her life easier, not more difficult. Now what was he to do?

"And now," she continued, breaking in on his thoughts once again, "as much as I would like to avoid making the acquaintance of a man of Lord Dunford's reputation, I really must continue to the hunting box."

Somehow, her comment took him by surprise. "You do not wish to know him?"

"Of course not. Why should I? From what I have heard of him, he has done nothing since inheriting his title save gamble the nights away and make a name for himself with his excesses. In all honesty, can you find anything in those two accomplishments that would make a person wish to know him?"

Mercifully, the question proved rhetorical, for she continued without waiting for Rand's reply. "Be that as it may, I must meet him, for I will not breathe easily until I have placed the little sailboat into the hand of Lord Care-For-Naught."

Lord Care-for-Naught. Rand had heard that appellation before, and though it was no more than the truth, he disliked hearing the term on Harriet Wilson's lips. For some reason, he hated knowing that she thought badly of him, even though she did not realize it *was* him.

"If it would help," he said, "I would be happy to

deliver the pin for you. As luck would have it, I am staying at Lord Dunford's hunting box."

"You are staying at—" She looked as if the words might choke her. "Sir! I had no idea you were a friend of his. Had I known, I would not have called him by that wretched name. Pray forgive my—"

"No apology necessary. Believe me, you cannot possibly call him something that he has not been called before."

"Even so, I should not have spoken. I have come all this way for no other reason than to protect my own reputation, and yet I have done unto Lord Dunford what I feared would be done unto me." She sighed. "What a hypocrite you must think me; for I judged his lordship on the strength of hearsay alone—gossip that might well be nothing more than fabrication."

She was silent for a time, busy examining a minuscule particle of lint on the sleeve of her York tan pelisse. Finally, she looked at Rand again. "If Lord Dunford is a friend of yours," she said quietly, "I am persuaded he cannot be so very bad."

The naive remark took Rand by surprise. It was clearly a compliment, albeit a paradoxical one. While he pondered how he should react to being thought a wastrel on one hand and a paragon on the other, she surprised him again. "Forgive me, sir, but I still do not know your name."

My name. Now what should he do? To tell her the truth now would certainly cause her embarrassment. It might even prompt her to give him the cut direct, and that was something he definitely did not want.

Stalling for time, he said, "It was by your own choice, ma'am, that I withheld that bit of information."

"Guilty as accused; for when we first met, I refused

to allow you to tell me your name. The situation is different now. We are both visiting in Kipworth, which is a small village, and since I plan to remain here for a sennight, there is every possibility that we shall meet again."

"I can almost guarantee it," he said.

She smiled then, and on the instant Rand decided to delay for as long as possible the revelation of his true identity.

"For my part," she said, "after your very glowing description of St. Agnes's, I am persuaded that I have but to mention the place to my cousins and they will insist that we give it a thorough perusal as soon as possible."

"Devotees of the antiquities, are they?"

To his delight, she smothered a giggle. "Perhaps not as much as you, sir. But, then, they are both rather young."

"How young?"

"Miles is ten, and his sister is seventeen."

"Ah, members of the infantry. That being true, there is but one thing we can do. We must tempt them to endure the touring of St. Agnes's by promising a visit afterward to a little baker's shop that boasts the lightest tea cakes in all of Leicestershire."

"Surely you know, sir, that all bakers claim to produce the lightest tea cakes in their particular shire?"

"In this instance, I promise you, the boast is true. Why, when I was a lad and wanted a second helping, I did not bother the baker's wife to bring me more of the cakes. I merely caught one or two as they floated by on the air."

She tried to maintain a somber face, but the corners of her mouth twitched just the least bit, encouraging Rand to pursue his advantage. "I saw that smile! Confess it, ma'am, you will have no rest until you have seen those floating cookies for yourself."

To his delight, she did not dissemble or turn miss-ish. "We have no plans for tomorrow," she said, "and my cousins and I would be delighted if you would act as our guide."

"Wonderful. Shall I stop by the Rose and Crown at eleven?"

"Eleven it is. And now, since I can assure you that my cousins will think it odd in the extreme if I intro-duce you merely as the gentleman whose quick thinking spared me a very nasty accident, you must tell me your name."

Deciding that a lie of omission might be easier to forgive at some later date than a lie of commission, he said, "My name is Randolph."

"Mr. Randolph," she said, offering him her hand, "I look forward to seeing you tomorrow. In the meantime, would you be so good as to see if you can separate that dear, sweet donkey from the apple trees, so that I may continue my journey to his lord-ship's hunting box?"

"I will do what I can to extricate the donkey, Miss Wilson. Unfortunately, I am afraid there would be no point in your continuing to the hunting box, not if your mission is to put the brooch in his lordship's hand. He is not there just at the moment."

She closed her eyes, as if to shield from view the degree of her disappointment. "Not there? Are you certain?"

"Quite."

"Drat the man! Must I spend my life pursuing him?"

"Certainly not. In fact, if I may offer a suggestion, I think it would be easier for all concerned if I ex-plained the circumstances of your errand to Lord Dunford and asked him to come to you at the inn."

While she considered his suggestion, Rand contin-ued. "I know for a fact that he rides daily, and it would be no bother for him to stop in at the Rose and Crown. Unless, of course, you actually enjoy pitting your will against that of yonder donkey. I hesitate to deprive you of what might be an enjoyable experience—"

"Deprive me, sir, please! Though I have been called stubborn on more than one occasion, when compared to that apple-eating beast, I am serenity personified. Furthermore, I venture to say that the less time I spend in the donkey's company, the more sunny my disposition will be."

After bestowing upon Rand a smile of genuine sweetness, she added, "Thank you for speaking to his lordship on my behalf. You are very kind."

Embarrassed as much by his own duplicity as by her unearned praise, Rand almost told her the truth. *Almost.* "Or," he said, "I would be happy to deliver the jewelry for you, Miss Wilson. That is, if you trust me with—"

"It is not a matter of trust!"

Harriet had never been so embarrassed in her life. She had brought this man into her home. Stood before him in nothing save her night rail and wrapper. She had even allowed him to kiss her. And now, after he had saved her life, she risked insulting him, and all because she insisted on personally placing the brooch in Lord Dunford's hand.

Before she could think what to say, he removed the necessity by reiterating his proposal to deliver the message to Lord Dunford. "Once that is done, Miss Wilson, I shall spend the remainder of the day in anticipation of the pleasure in store for me tomorrow, when I show you and your cousins the wonders of Kipworth."

Rand had spoken truthfully when he said he looked forward to their outing. Though there were few in London who would credit that Lord Care-For-Naught would bestir himself on behalf of two young people and a female no longer in her first blush of youth, he found he liked the idea more with each passing minute.

"What can you tell me?" he asked his brother that evening, interrupting what had thus far been a totally silent meal, "of the attractions one might show a visitor to Kipworth?"

Though Burton looked up from his plate, the sullen expression on his face did not change. "What sort of visitor?"

Rand hesitated an instant before answering. "A lady."

"One of your doxies, do you mean? Take her to the alehouse and ply her with strong drink. It should make your conquest that much easier."

"The visitor is a *lady*," he repeated through clenched teeth.

"A thousand pardons," Burton said, "for having jumped to conclusions." Feigning boredom, he lifted his napkin to his lips as if to cover a yawn. "One has to wonder, though, why a lady would agree to spend time in your company."

Though Rand refused to dignify the remark with a reply, the attempt to curb his anger had ruined his appetite, prompting him to push aside the plate that contained his uneaten fish course. Lifting the wineglass the footman had only just refilled, he downed the contents.

"Is her family hard-pressed for money?" Burton asked. "When families meet with fiscal reverses, I believe it is often expected that the daughter of the house sacrifice herself for the greater good by going on the catch for a wealthy husband. If the wind is in that direction, I can only hope *the lady* has a strong stomach. Have you mentioned Belle Coombs to her?"

"Enough, you blasted puppy! For your own sake, I advise you to keep a civil tongue in your head."

In the past four days, Rand had tried everything he knew to introduce some topic that would lead to genial conversation between him and his brother. If they could establish some sort of friendly rapport, perhaps Burton would come to trust him enough to tell him about the Wexham brothers and their threat.

So far, nothing had worked, and Rand's patience was wearing thin. Burton refused every overture of friendship, and though he had washed, donned clean clothes, and appeared quite sober, his stubborn refusal to let go of the prejudice he had nurtured for twelve years put Rand in mind of Miss Wilson's donkey.

Trying one last time, he said, "The lady of whom I speak is in Kipworth for a sennight's holiday, she and her two cousins. I offered to escort them to St. Agnes's, but I cannot think a boy of ten will find much to interest him in a Norman church."

A bark of laughter, though intended as a scoff, told Rand he was correct. "Since you are not so very many years older than the lad, Burton, not to mention being more familiar with any recent changes in the village, I had hoped that you might advise me. Do you think you might swallow the animosity you bear me, just for a minute or two? Just long enough to answer a civil question?"

Burton pushed aside his own plate, then signaled to the footman to replenish his glass. Unfortunately, at an almost imperceptible shake of his master's head, the servant pretended a sudden loss of vision and trained his gaze on the far wall.

"Devil take it! I will not be treated like a child."

"Then do not act like one."

Apparently hearing the steel in his older brother's voice, Burton propped his elbows on the table, rested his chin in his palms, then started petulantly at his empty glass. After a time, he said, "Take the brat to Bosworth Field. Small boys are always happy to visit battle sites."

The suggestion, though spoken in a surly manner, was a good one, a circumstance that tempered Rand's reply. "I had forgotten about Bosworth Field. Thank you. I will ask the lady about it tomorrow."

"Chances are she will find it a dead bore. Nothing much there but an open field. However, if you set to memory a few lines from Shakespeare's *Richard The Third,* and whisper them in her ear, she will probably end the day by swooning at your feet. Females like that sort of thing."

Rand could not decide which amused him most, the idea of taking advice about the fair sex from his nineteen-year-old brother, or the thought of beguiling Harriet Wilson with a whispered recitation of, "A horse, a horse, my kingdom for a horse." In any event, he hid his smile, unwilling to put an end to what he hoped was the beginning of a truce.

"If I remember correctly, the battle site is some five or six miles distance. For such a journey, I should think an open chaise would be best. Where is the most reliable place to hire such a conveyance?"

Burton shrugged his shoulders, as if already tiring of the subject. "There is an old, yet serviceable landau in your own stables. If you order it cleaned up, it should do well enough for the journey."

"Excellent. And what of a meal? Is there a respectable inn nearby where the ladies might refresh themselves?"

"There is, but I do not recall the name of the place. Perhaps I should come along to show you the way."

The moment the words left his mouth, Burton longed to bite his tongue. What on earth had possessed him to make such an idiotic suggestion? A visit to Bosworth Field would take the better part of a day, and the last thing he wanted was to spend more time in Rand's company. And judging by the guarded look that came into his older brother's eyes, he was equally displeased by the prospect.

"Thank you," Rand said, "but I am certain I can find the place. Besides, the ladies would be uncomfortable with more than four in the landau."

Aha! Burton had been correct in his surmise. His older brother definitely did not want him to come along, a fact that piqued his interest. "Plenty of horses in the stables. I could always ride."

"Another time," Rand said, looking not at Burton, but at a small spot on the white damask table cover. "Thank you, though, for the offer."

When Rand immediately laid his napkin on the table, excused himself from the meal, then exited the dining room, it was obvious that his purpose was to put a stop to any further discussion of the proposed trip. Burton found this behavior intriguing. For some reason, his brother did not want him tagging along on the excursion, and the only explanation that presented itself was that he did not want Burton to meet this mysterious lady.

He could not imagine why this should be so, especially if she *was* a lady. Not that it mattered, for on the instant Burton decided that no force in nature would stop him from riding to the village the next day. He was fascinated by the prospect of doing something to annoy, perhaps even embarrass the big brother whose actions had besmirched the Dunford name.

"A sweet idea!" he muttered, surprising the footman who immediately grabbed up a tray containing servings of fruit pie with clotted cream and a chantilly cake flanked by a dish of sack cream. "No, no," Burton said, waving aside the tray. He refused even to consider one of the sweets, for he was much more interested in "Just deserts."

Smiling at his own pun, he pushed back his chair and stood. "This should prove interesting," he said, not caring if anyone heard him. "After all, it has been years since I visited St. Agnes's."

Chapter Six

The next morning, after the three cousins had broken their fasts in their private dining room, Harriet left word with the innkeeper that they were expecting company. "The gentleman's name is Randolph. Would you be so kind as to send word up to Sir Miles's chamber the moment Mr. Randolph arrives?"

"Of course, Miss Wilson."

Thanking the man, Harriet turned to go to her own chamber for her bonnet and gloves. Her foot had no more than touched the bottom stair when someone tapped her on the arm. "Excuse me."

Thinking she must have dropped something, Harriet paused, turning expectantly. "Yes?"

"Miss Wilson?"

The female, who had arrived at the inn only moments before, was dressed in a blue faille traveling costume that was undoubtedly the work of one of London's top mantua makers. Even so, the beautifully cut dress and spencer did not quite disguise the fact that she was taller than average and a bit on the thin side. Her age might have been anything between thirty-five and forty, and though Harriet met many people in her line of work, she was reasonably certain she was unacquainted with this particular female.

Ever alert to the possibility of a new jewelry commission, especially from one whose personal traveling coach was even now being driven around to the rear of the inn yard, Harriet smiled hopefully. "Good morning, ma'am. Forgive me, but are we acquainted?"

"No, no," the newcomer said, shaking her head and causing a veritable fluttering of the dyed gold grebe feathers that adorned the edges of her blue silk hat. "We have never met, Miss Wilson. And it's me as should be begging your pardon, for speaking to you in what you must think a thoroughly coming manner."

For a moment, Harriet had been misled by the elegance of the woman's coach, by her expensive clothes, and by the expertly coiffed curls that framed the sides of her face, assuming she was part of the *ton*, a lady on her way home to her country estate. On her way to an estate she might be. Wealthy she might be. But from the broad Yorkshire in her speech, it was obvious that whoever she was, she was not a member of the *ton*.

"I could not help overhearing your conversation with the innkeeper," she said. "And when I heard you mention someone called Sir Miles, I knew I had to speak to you, to discover if you referred to Sir Miles Gwynn, a young gentleman whose uncle is Mr. Frederick Gwynn?"

The woman's plain face appeared open and honest, but Harriet had learned long ago that people were not always what they seemed. For that reason, she answered the question with one of her own. "Are you acquainted with Mr. Frederick Gwynn?"

"I have that pleasure, ma'am. Mr. Gwynn and I met in town several weeks ago, at Vauxhall Gardens."

"At Vauxhall?" Still unsure how to proceed, Harriet said, "And Mr. Gwynn is well?"

"Quite well, ma'am, as you will soon be able to

see for yourself. As it happens, I have every reason to believe that he will be stopping at this very inn within the next day or so."

Frederick Gwynn here? At the Rose and Crown? Silently Harriet cursed the man for his ill timing. He had obviously been in town for weeks without calling upon his niece and nephew, to inquire how they got on, and now here he was about to present himself in Kipworth, of all places.

As her mother's sister's brother-in-law, Frederick was a mere connection to Harriet, and he had no power to influence her comings and goings. He was, however, the uncle and legal guardian of Miles and Anna. Never a downy fellow at the best of times, if he should suddenly take it into his head to begin exerting his legal rights, he could insist that Harriet take her cousins back to London immediately.

Twenty-four hours ago, Harriet would not have taken such an order amiss; after all, she had come to Leicestershire on an errand, with no notion of enjoying her time here. But twenty-four hours ago she had not known that Mr. Randolph was visiting in the neighborhood. Nor could she have guessed at the pleasure it would give her to renew her acquaintance with the tall, handsome gentleman—a gentleman whose teasing ways and wicked smile made her heart react as though it belonged in the chest of some giddy schoolroom chit.

"As it happens," the woman said, the tone of her voice all but daring Harriet to question her actions, "Mr. Gwynn's future presence is my motive for stopping at this inn."

Her attention caught, Harriet was forced to abandon her daydreaming about Mr. Randolph and the delight she felt just knowing she would soon spend several hours in his company. She had missed some of what the woman had been saying, but now she wished she had been attending. "Your pardon, ma'am, for I must have been woolgathering. Would you be so kind as to repeat what you just said?"

"I was saying that I stopped at the Rose and Crown for no other reason than to allow Mr. Gwynn time to catch up with me."

The audacity of the admission left Harriet all but speechless. "Catch up with you?"

The woman nodded. "I have every reason to believe that he is traveling north for only one purpose, to ask my father for my hand in marriage."

Harriet schooled her face to show no reaction, but she had trouble imagining this strong-willed female married to a man whose resolve and intellect were not remarkable, and whose only claim to distinction was his impeccable taste in waistcoats.

"I know what you are thinking, Miss Wilson."

"You do?"

"You are thinking that I must be mistaken about Mr. Gwynn's intentions. Knowing him as you do, you are probably thinking as well that a gentleman of his address and connections could have any young lady he chose."

"I assure you, ma'am, I was thinking nothing of the kind."

If Harriet had been inclined to share her thoughts with this stranger, she would have mentioned that Frederick Gwynn was forty if he was a day and already losing the battle against corpulence. Furthermore, as a younger son he had no property of his own and only a small trust fund upon which to support himself. As a consequence, his pockets were almost always to let. To the parents of even the least popular young lady of the season, a gentleman of Frederick's age and financial circumstances was not looked on favorably as possible husband material.

"I've no wish to gammon you, Miss Wilson. With

me not being any good at dissembling, I'll be frank, if I may."

The request was obviously rhetorical, for she did not wait for permission before she continued. "You will understand Mr. Gwynn's initial interest in me when I tell you that my da is Homer Shaw, owner of two very prosperous coal mines."

Here was plain speaking indeed!

"Da is a widower, and I am his only child. My dowry is in excess of twenty thousand pounds, and as sole heiress to Da's property, I will one day be a very wealthy woman."

"How . . . How nice for you."

Harriet could not believe she was having this conversation. And with a complete stranger! Though she was engaged in commerce, she was nonetheless startled by this very frank discussion of finances. A true lady would never speak of money outside the privacy of her own home. If Miss Shaw was aware of having committed a faux pas, however, she gave no indication of it.

"The thing is, Miss Wilson, that Mr. Gwynn and I rub along together very nicely, and I think he is just the gentleman for me. He is easily swayed, however, and for that reason I feel it would be best if I had a few days alone with him before he meets my da. I want to see can I bring him to the sticking point before we reach my home."

Not a little astonished by the confession, Harriet could only stare. Thankfully, Miss Shaw did not appear to expect any comment. "Frederick being a gentleman," she continued, "I know he would never go back on his word once it was given. Just let me get his betrothal ring on my finger, and there will be no turning back, no matter how much my da might fuss and fume and try to turn him away."

Turn him away? Harriet could not believe that at

all likely. An heiress Miss Shaw might be, but she was no beauty, and she was well past her second, even her third blush of youth. Frederick Gwynn might not have a feather to fly with, as the saying went, but he had excellent *ton*, and he was accepted everywhere.

Furthermore, the members of society understood the necessity for replenishing depleted family coffers, and they would not fault Frederick for choosing the expedient route to solvency. Not that the advantages would be all on his side. An alliance with a man of his stamp would assure Miss Shaw entrée into all but the most exalted society, an acceptance she could gain in no other way. No, Harriet could not believe the woman's father would not see the advantages.

"My da is as good-hearted a man as the Heavenly Father ever made, but he's strongwilled for all that. And," she added, albeit self-consciously, "he's quite misguided as to the degree of my, er, beauty. He sent me to town with instructions to come home with a duke, or at the very least an earl."

Harriet very nearly laughed out loud. *A duke!* Not since the arrival of the celebrated Gunning sisters, both of whom were reputed to be females of incomparable beauty, had a nobody snared a duke.

"As you probably know," Miss Shaw said, "there just aren't all that many dukes and earls to go around, even for a female with twenty thousand and a future inheritance to sweeten the prospective alliance. Besides, I took an instant liking to Mr. Gwynn. He's ever so refined, and not a bit puffed up, for all he's a gentleman, and the son, brother, and uncle of a baronet. And," she added, running her gloved hand down the sleeve of her blue faille spencer, "he has excellent taste."

With that, at least, Harriet could agree.

"It was Mr. Gwynn who introduced me to Madame Ezelle's establishment, then helped me to select my new wardrobe."

Miss Shaw paused, and Harriet, perceiving that some comment was expected from her, said, "Very nice, ma'am. A most becoming blue."

"As my da would say, 'Fine feathers make fine birds.' I'm no beauty, Miss Wilson, and I know it, but from our first meeting, Mr. Gwynn saw something in me. Something he liked well enough to pursue the acquaintance."

Twenty thousand somethings, Harriet suspected, though she was careful not to give voice to that particular suspicion. Afraid she might say something unflattering about the gentleman, she steered the conversation to Miss Shaw's reason for speaking to her. "Was there something you wanted me to relate to Sir Miles? Something about his uncle, perhaps?"

"Only that his uncle should be arriving soon, and that I feel certain he will be pleased to see his niece and nephew. Though, to tell the truth, Miss Wilson, I suspect he will be quite surprised to discover them here."

Harriet could well believe it. Her hope was that the surprise did not prompt him to banish them on sight.

Sensing that Miss Shaw was not quite finished with what she wished to say, Harriet invited her to continue. "Somehow, ma'am, I feel the real purpose of this conversation has not yet been mentioned."

For the first time, Miss Shaw looked uncomfortable. "I'm nothing if not blunt, Miss Wilson, so I'll come right out with it. I hope—no, I pray—that neither you nor Sir Miles and his sister will try to influence Mr. Gwynn against me.

"I am an avid gardener, an occupation that takes up a goodly portion of my day. And though I am never happier than when my fingers are in the soil, or when I am in my greenhouse, developing new hybrids, it is not enough. I want a husband while there is still time enough for me to give him children."

She lowered her gaze momentarily. "You'll forgive me, Miss Wilson, if I have put you to the blush."

"No, no. Think nothing of it."

"You'll understand my reasons for wanting to keep Mr. Gwynn here until I have his declaration, when I tell you that my da has refused the only two offers I've had for my hand, on account of him wanting to see me elevated into the highest of society."

Returning her gaze to Harriet's face, she looked her directly in the eyes. "In all truthfulness, cutting a dash among the *ton* has never been a wish of mine. Never. So you need not be fearing, Miss Wilson, that I will be forever hanging on your sleeve, pestering you to take me about and introduce me to your friends."

More embarrassed than she had thought possible, Harriet assured her that nothing *she* could say would have the least influence upon the *ton*. "As for influencing Mr. Gwynn against you, you have my word that I will say nothing on the subject. I cannot, of course, speak for Anna and Miles, but as you will see for yourself, they are sweet-tempered and unassuming young people, and I am persuaded they would do nothing counter to their uncle's best interests."

Thankfully, this unusual tête à tête was interrupted by the arrival of Mr. Randolph, who merely stepped inside the inn door and waited politely for Harriet to notice him.

And notice him she did! Even if she had not seen him dismount his horse and hand the chestnut into the keeping of the waiting ostler, Harriet would have known he was on the premises. The acceleration of her heartbeats would have told her he was near.

He looked even handsomer than she remembered, and the sight of him, so tall, and so totally masculine in a snug-fitting corbeau green coat and biscuit-colored breeches, made her long to hurry to him so that not a minute of their afternoon together was wasted. Aware that such unseemly exuberance might make him wish he had not promised to be their guide for the day, she merely nodded to him. "I shall be but a moment, sir. I must fetch my bonnet."

"Oh," Miss Shaw said, staring from Harriet to Mr. Randolph, then back to Harriet, a look of surprise on her face. "I, er, see you are promised elsewhere, Miss Wilson, so I will detain you no longer."

Harriet made some sort of reply—what it was she neither knew nor cared—then she made her excuses and hurried up the stairs. She was just turning to make her way down the narrow, timber-framed corridor leading to her bedchamber when she heard Miss Shaw speak to Mr. Randolph.

"Good day to you, my lord."

"Ma'am," he replied.

Sparing a thought for poor Miss Shaw, Harriet decided it was as well that the mine owner's daughter did not wish to make her way among the *ton*. Especially if she did not even know enough not to call a plain mister "my lord."

The short walk from the Rose and Crown to St. Agnes's Church took the foursome across the village green with its grazing sheep, and beyond that bucolic spot past the bakery, a dressmaker's shop, and a four-story structure whose sign declared it to be the Simpson Glove Manufactory. To the surprise of neither of the ladies, the leisurely stroll was enlivened by a spate of questions from Miles, who had contracted an instantaneous and rather severe case of hero worship for Mr. Randolph.

Starved for male companionship, Miles had not left the gentleman's side since the moment Harriet made the introductions. Now, as they passed the saddlery, then a butcher's shop, where four fat ducks had been hung in the open doorway to entice customers, the lad asked about the natives of the islands. "Are they hostile, sir?"

"The Caribs? No. Not at all," he said. Then, at the lad's sigh of disappointment, he added rather hastily, "But, of course, one must be ever watchful of the pirates that abound in the area."

"Pirates! Truly, sir?"

"Oh, my, yes. One has but to walk the beaches to see the Jolly Roger outlined against the horizon, the skull and crossbones waving ominously in the breeze. Trade winds, you know. You have, I presume, learned of the trade winds in your studies?"

"Apparently not so much as I should have, sir, but I mean to remedy that oversight the moment we return to town."

"I am happy to hear it, my boy, for such knowledge is an absolute necessity." Dropping his voice to a dramatic whisper, he said, "In truth, a man never knows when such information may become a matter of life and death."

"Life and death," Miles repeated, his own voice hushed with awe.

For Harriet's part, she was obliged to hide her smile, for though she had heard that pirate ships found sanctuary in the islands, she doubted very much that their dreaded mascots were in evidence all that often. Still, she thanked the gentleman silently for the manner in which he caught Miles's interest, then turned the conversation to his studies.

With the distant church spire as their beacon, the ladies led the way up a slight incline. Since the width of the pavement allowed for no more than two abreast, the gentlemen had chosen to follow, but they were close enough for Harriet to hear question number one thousand and one from Miles. "How long were you in the Caribbean, sir?"

Though Harriet detected a hint of reserve in their guide's voice when he spoke of his time in Barbados, she did not think what she heard was impatience with Miles's questions. In fact, the gentleman was being unbelievably patient, almost as if he understood the lad's need for a male he could look up to, and Harriet could not begin to say what his forbearance meant to her.

No more than she could say how relieved she had been earlier that morning, back at the inn, in the moments following her introduction of the lovely Anna to Mr. Randolph.

As luck would have it, Miss Anna Gwynn had looked even more beautiful than usual, artlessly attired in a yellow sprigged muslin that showed her pretty figure to perfection and a gypsy hat that sat innocently atop her fair curls. No less eager than her brother to begin their exploration of the area, her excitement at the prospect of adventure was reflected in her eyes, which resembled nothing so much as priceless sapphires. Even Miles had noticed his sister's beauty, going so far as to express his hope that she would refrain from turning too many heads.

As for Mr. Randolph, like all those of his sex, he had stood practically speechless upon first spying the young lady. To Harriet's immense relief, however, he had made Anna a polite bow, shaken her brother's hand, then turned immediately to their cousin. "Now there," he said to the latter, "is a young lady who will not be long on the marriage mart."

"No," Harriet agreed, "for she is very beautiful."

"Damned with faint praise," he replied, sending

Harriet's heart plummeting to her feet, "for the chit is an absolute picture. A diamond of the first water. A true incomparable."

Harriet almost choked on what was truly her first pang of jealousy. Obliged to swallow several times to ease the knot in her throat, she wondered how she would get through the day if Mr. Randolph aligned himself with all Anna's other admirers.

"She is perfection," he continued, "no doubt about it." Then, just as Harriet was about to turn away, lest he read the disappointment on her face, he leaned toward her, speaking low, his words for her ear only. "Though honesty compels me to admit that for a man of my advanced years, perfection can be a bit trying."

Her spirits miraculously on the mend, Harriet said, "Your advanced years? I had not thought you all that old, sir."

"Oh, but I am, Miss Wilson. And for that reason, if I am to be long in a lady's company, she must know the value of a flaw."

"A flaw?"

"Two would be even better."

At his teasing tone, Harriet felt the return of the day's promised pleasure. "If I may ask, sir, what sort of flaw do you require?"

As if needing to ponder the matter, he hesitated for a moment. "Any number of possibilities come to mind, but I should think a willingness to do murder would serve. In fact, I know a certain donkey cart driver with that very flaw."

"Do you, now?"

"And as it happens," he added, giving her a smile that turned the bones in her knees to India rubber, "that same murderous lady has another rather noticeable imperfection."

"She does?" Harriet hoped her voice did not sound

as breathless as she felt. "Pray, what is that imperfection?"

"Her smile," he said. "It is just the least bit crooked."

"Crooked! No such thing."

"Afraid so, ma'am. Definitely aslant. Surely you have noticed it on those occasions when you gaze overlong into your looking glass."

"Overlong into my— Sir! I will have you know that I am not so conceited as to—"

Realizing she had risen to the bait, Harriet clamped her lips shut. Immediately, he gave her one of those smiles that belonged by right to the lord of the underworld, and unable to stop herself, she responded with a smile of her own.

"There! There it is," he said. "The right corner of your mouth turns up just the slightest bit more than the left. If I may say so, a perfect flaw."

"Perfect flaw? Forgive me, sir, but unless I am mistaken, that is an oxymoron."

"Oh, dear," he said. "Never tell me you are a bluestocking as well. That makes three flaws. Keep them coming, Miss Wilson. I vow I am feeling better by the minute."

Though hard-pressed not to laugh at his foolishness, Harriet decided they had spoken in private long enough. Their tête à tête had already earned her a number of speculative glances from other of the inn's patrons, and not wanting to figure as the day's topic of conversation, she bid her cousins come along so they could be on their way.

"Actually," Mr. Randolph said, answering another of Miles's questions and bringing Harriet's thoughts back to the present, "I found sea travel most enjoyable. But, of course, my experience is as a passenger. From what I witnessed, I do not think that life is very comfortable for the members of the crew. Therefore, if you are thinking of taking up pirating as a lifestyle, my boy, I should warn you against it. Weeks at sea, hard labor, and poor food are but a few of the trials a seaman must endure."

"But, sir," Miles said, unwilling to forsake his romantic vision of life at sea, "only think of the adventures even an ordinary sailor must have."

"Right you are, lad. The adventures must be endless. Endless hours of swabbing the deck. Endless mornings spent emptying the rat traps. Endless afternoons spent bailing out the bilgewater. And let us not forget the ever-present weevils in the biscuits and the green scum on the surface of the drinking water. High adventure indeed."

Anna shuddered, and Harriet, who had partaken of a substantial breakfast, begged Miles to change the subject to one more felicitous to the digestion. Since they had just passed the apothecary's shop—the last establishment on the high street—and were approaching the stacked stone wall that surrounded the churchyard, nothing more was said until they had passed through the open gate, then traversed the cobblestone path that led up to the door of St. Agnes's Church.

Harriet was so intent on searching for the little brass plaque Mr. Randolph had mentioned, the one to the right of the thick, battered old door, that she almost collided with a slender young gentleman who had just stepped out of the church. "I beg your pardon, sir."

"My fault entirely," the gentleman said. "I fear I was not attending—" He stopped midsentence, for at that moment he spied Anna Gwynn and was, for all practical purposes, turned to a statue.

While the young man stood thus, his mouth agape and his expression resembling that of a person whose senses had gone wanting, Mr. Randolph and Miles caught up with Harriet and Anna.

"Burton!" Mr. Randolph said, glowering at the newcomer. "What the deuce are you doing here?"

Finding his voice at last, the young man stammered a reply of sorts. "I, er . . . Rand! I say. What a surprise to find you here!"

Chapter Seven

Realizing that introductions were unavoidable, Rand stepped forward. "Miss Wilson," he said, "Miss Anna Gwynn, Sir Miles. May I present Mr. Burton Dunford? Burton is the brother of my host at the hunting lodge."

Another lie of omission added to the ever-growing list.

Rand looked from his brother to Miss Wilson, unsure which of them would react first at the mention of his supposed host. Thankfully, his brother was too taken with gazing at Miss Anna Gwynn to notice the peculiarity of the introduction. As for Miss Wilson, her only reaction was a slight intake of breath.

Silently she studied Burton, as if to determine if he was to be tarred with the same brush as his older brother. Apparently deciding to give the young man the benefit of the doubt, she extended her hand. "How do you do, Mr. Dunford? Mr. Randolph was so kind as to offer to act as our guide through the church. Have you already seen it, or would you care to join us?"

Burton took the proffered hand and bowed over it. He had snapped out of his stupor in time to hear the last part of the lady's comment, and since what he heard included an invitation to join her and her exquisite charge, he readily agreed to the scheme. In his nineteen years, he had never beheld a creature more beautiful than Miss Anna Gwynn, and after seeing her, he had no difficulty in guessing his brother's *real* reason for coming to Kipworth.

So much for his supposed big-brotherly concern!

Though Burton had no way of knowing if Rand's intentions toward the beauty were honorable or otherwise, it was obvious that this was the "lady" he had mentioned last evening at dinner. No wonder he was at such pains to discover something that would keep her little brother entertained. Rand had his eye on the lovely Miss Gwynn, and obviously the way into her good graces was through her young brother.

Of course, the lady was rather young herself. A good age for a gentleman of nineteen, but much too young for Rand. Never mind his brother's sullied reputation; even without it, he was too old for this angel.

Deciding on the instant that the honor of his family depended upon his doing all within his power to thwart Rand's nefarious plans, Burton offered the young lady his arm. "May I, Miss Gwynn?"

"Why, thank you," she replied, bestowing upon him a smile so sweet, so angelic, that he wondered how he ever could have thought himself in love with a female as unrefined as Flo Wexham, the tavern keeper's daughter.

"My pleasure," he said.

As he led the beauty into the peaceful old sanctuary, Burton was obliged to hide his smile, knowing he had gotten the better of his brother at last. By his quick thinking, he had claimed Miss Gwynn's company for himself, thereby forcing Rand to escort the other, rather plain lady instead.

To Rand's relief, his brother was too dumbfounded by the beautiful Miss Gwynn to notice much of anything that was said during the following hour. In fact, the visit to St. Agnes's went rather well, with Burton needing only one rather emphatic jab to the ribs to stop him from revealing Rand's true identity.

"At that time," Burton said, answering Anna's question as to when he had lost his parents, "I was still at Eton."

"Poor lad," she said, her eyes pooling with tears of sincere sympathy. "How fortunate that you had the support of your brother."

"Actually, my brother was not here. He was still in Barba— Ooph!"

"The walls of this edifice are Norman," Rand said rather hurriedly, stepping away from his wounded brother, "and they were constructed at some time during the thirteenth century. And yet," he added, indicating the long, narrow central hall of the cruciform church, "the nave is pure Saxon, built, I believe in the eleventh century."

Miss Wilson had been examining a small stained-glass window depicting Richard the Third standing beside his fallen horse, but at Rand's impromptu lecture she turned toward him, a smile on her lips. "So, you have decided to try your hand at instructing. Pray, do not forget about the Roman ruins," she said. "I should dislike it of all things if our guide ran out of erudite remarks before we quit this lovely old structure."

"Minx!" he whispered. "I can see that you would like nothing better than to prove me a humbug."

"Oh, no, sir. I depend upon you doing that for yourself, without any assistance from me."

He chuckled, delighted at her quickness. He enjoyed her company more with each meeting. Unlike most of the females of his acquaintance, she was open and honest with her feelings, displaying not the first sign of duplicity or guile. She enjoyed being with him, too—or rather, with plain Mr. Randolph—and she did not attempt to hide the fact.

And for his part, Rand relished being liked for himself. It was a new experience. Since returning to England as Lord Dunford, he had met with two types of behavior: a fawning sycophancy from people who wanted something from him, and total rebuff from his brother.

Harriet Wilson fit into neither of those categories.

From the outset, she had offered him the hand of friendship with no strings attached, and because it had been a long time since he'd had a friend, he had accepted. She was brave and honest, and unlike him, she had not allowed adversity to harden her. He liked her, and he was human enough not to want to see the disappointment in her eyes once she discovered that he was Lord Dunford.

Thinking only to delay that look for as long as possible, he stayed within hearing of his brother so he could interrupt if Burton should say anything else that might reveal his true identity. Fortunately, nothing more was said of his lordship, and only after they had enjoyed a delightful tea at the bakery, then returned to the Rose and Crown, was his name mentioned again.

While they stood in the inn yard, making arrangements for the following day's outing to Bosworth Field, Rand asked Miles if he would inform the ostler that he was ready for his horse.

"Of course, sir."

The lad had only just set off at a run when Burton noticed the smaller of the two signs above the inn door. "By Jove," he said. "What is today?"

"Tuesday," Anna replied. "Why do you ask?"

He pointed to the sign. "Would that make day after tomorrow the lecture and recital Thursday or the Thursday for the subscription assemblies?"

After a moment's thought, the young lady smiled. "The assembly, I believe. Which would you prefer it to be, Mr. Dunford?"

"The assembly, of course. That is, if you mean to attend, Miss Gwynn."

She looked to her cousin for guidance, but Miss Wilson's attention was caught by Miles, who hurried toward her, a letter in his hand. "Cousin Harriet," he said, breathless as much from excitement as from his run, "this is for you."

"For me? But who—"

"Someone left it with the ostler," he said. "And it must be important, for the gentleman gave the ostler an entire guinea to be certain he delivered the letter to you the moment you returned from St. Agnes's."

"A guinea? As you say, it must be important. But who could have . . ." The lady said no more, but from the look on her face, she was worried by the unexpectedness of the communication. After excusing herself to the group, she tore open the wafer, then unfolded the single sheet.

"Nothing so very distressing, I hope," Rand said.

"No, praise heaven. Though for a minute I feared it might be bad news from home. Instead, it is a message from Lord Dunford."

"Dunford?" Immediately suspicious, Burton looked directly at Rand, whose face was unreadable. "What can my brother be up to now, I wonder, leaving letters for ostlers to deliver?" Returning his gaze to Miss Wilson, he said, "Somehow, ma'am, I had settled it in my mind that you and Dunford were unacquainted."

"You were correct, sir, for his lordship and I are strangers. As you can imagine, we travel in vastly different circles, so our paths have never crossed."

"Never? How odd, to be sure. It being such a small world and all."

Rand cleared his throat, and as he did so, he gave Burton a look that said this day's work would not go unchallenged. "How unfortunate," he said, "that you missed Lord Dunford once again, Miss Wilson. Did he, perchance, mention your errand?"

She nodded. "He writes that he was sorry to have missed me, and he asks that I give the brooch into your keeping, Mr. Randolph. He goes on to mention his appreciation for what he calls my conscientiousness; then he closes by saying that I am to think no more of the matter."

"Which suggestion," Rand said, "I hope you will follow. That silly piece of jewelry has consumed way too much of your time already."

She made no reply to his remark. After refolding the letter, she merely asked him if he would be so good as to wait while she fetched the brooch. At his nod of assent, she excused herself and hurried inside the inn and up the stairs. Within a matter of minutes she had returned with a small, black velvet bag, which she gave to him.

Placing her warm, soft fingers over his, she spoke quietly, for his ears only. "Will you do something for me, my friend?"

"Anything. You have but to name it."

"I know I am being foolish, but for my peace of mind, will you place this directly into Lord Dunford's hand?"

"Consider it done, Miss Wilson."

After leaving the inn yard, Rand kept the chestnut at a walk for most of the two-mile trip back to the hunting box. He had hoped his brother would gallop on ahead, but for some reason Burton kept his horse's pace even with that of the chestnut's. For once, however, he had the good sense to keep his mouth shut.

Rand needed silence in which to arrange his thoughts—thoughts that were chaotic to say the least. From the moment Harriet had put that small velvet bag in his hand, then closed her fingers over his and placed her trust in him as her friend, he had been experiencing feelings he had thought long vanished from his soul. And the feeling that took precedence was, for want of a better word, remorse.

What was it about the woman that stirred the embers of a conscience he had thought long burned out of him?

In order to survive the past twelve years, he had committed any number of less than honorable acts, committed them without even a hint of regret. So how was it that just seeing the trust in those pansy eyes, and hearing her call him her friend, had made Rand long for some magical river in which to submerge himself—one whose waters would wash him clean of all his past deeds?

And not just those from his past, for he was lying to her even now. Let him call them sins of omission; the truth was still the truth and a lie was still a lie. And once Harriet Wilson discovered who and what he was, the result would be the same. She would never believe that he had meant her no harm.

She would withdraw her friendship, and when she did so, Rand was certain he would lose what little remained of the gentle young man who had once lived inside him.

At the moment, however, the thing he was in danger of losing was his hearing. His brother was talking to him, and Rand was so deep in thought, wondering how he was to extricate himself from the tangle of lies, that he had not heard the first word. "Therefore," Burton said, "I felt I must say what was on my mind. In good conscience, I cannot remain silent."

From the tone of his voice, the ride from the village

had given him just enough time to work up his anger. Rand tried to control his own displeasure, for at the moment he was in no mood to indulge any of his brother's grievances. "What now, Burton?"

"It is about the lady."

Rand was surprised by the sudden introduction of the subject foremost in his own thoughts. After the besotted way his brother had ogled Miss Gwynn, he had not thought Burton even noticed Harriet Wilson. "What about the lady?"

Burton hesitated, and for a moment Rand thought he meant to let the subject drop. He was mistaken, however, for his brother drew a deep breath, as if to fortify himself for an argument, then blurted out what was on his mind. "Just that she *is* a lady."

"And?"

"And," Burton said, the single word filled with contempt, "even a man of your stamp must know when a female is beyond his touch."

The remark being indisputable, Rand made no reply. He was wondering where this conversation was leading when a bullet suddenly *zinged* past his head, missing him by mere inches. The chestnut was the first to react, squealing in fright and raising up on its hind legs.

For several seconds, it was all Rand could do to keep the gelding from bolting. "Mercury!" he called, trying to calm the startled animal. "Steady on. Easy does it. There's a good boy."

The report of the pistol had startled Burton's horse as well, though not as violently, and for a minute Rand thought his brother would give the horse his head and let him gallop on home. In this, at least, he had misjudged the younger man, for once Burton had calmed his mount, he waited only for Mercury to settle down before rejoining Rand.

"Damnation!" Burton said. "That was close. Are you injured?"

Rand shook his head. "Did you see who fired the shot?"

"No, but I daresay the fellow is halfway to Newcastle by now, and still running. Chances are he was as startled as we were by the mishap. I shouldn't worry overmuch about him. Probably nothing more than some poacher after a pheasant."

Or some Frenchman after my hide!

The shot had come from a pistol, not from a fowling piece. Rand heard the difference even if his brother did not. Though he decided to say nothing more of the matter for the moment, he fully intended to write to Bow Street, where runners were supposedly keeping an eye on the movement of Antoine de la Croix.

At just that moment, the yelping of the hounds in the kennels brought Rand's thoughts back to his surroundings. The horses' hooves sounded on the crushed-stone carriageway, and by the time the brothers reached the shallow overhang at the entrance to the hunting box, a groom had come at a run from the stables.

The servant was just leading the animals away when Burton returned to the subject that had been interrupted by the shot. "About the lady," he began. "She—"

"Enough!" Rand said. More than a little rattled by how close he had come to losing his life, he was in no mood to argue. Instead, he walked past Burton and up the stairs that led to his bedchamber.

"You leave her be!" Burton yelled after him. "She is too fine, too lovely for the likes of you."

Rand did not even look back. For once, he and his brother were in complete agreement.

Unfortunately, the same could not be said for Miss Eunice Shaw and her hopeful swain, Mr. Frederick Gwynn. For the past half hour, since the plump,

middle-aged gentleman's arrival at the Rose and
Crown, the two had sat beside the small fire lit in
the common room, in total disagreement with one
another. "Stap my vitals! You must be mistaken,
Eunice."

"But I tell you, Freddy, I saw his lordship with my
own eyes. We even exchanged greetings. True, we've
never been introduced, me not traveling in such exalted circles, but when I was in town, he was pointed
out to me on more than one occasion."

"But I have it on good account that Dunford never
leaves the clubs and gaming hells. Not even to visit
his estates. That being so, why on earth would a man
of his stamp—one who likes the excitement of town
and heavy play—be whiling away his hours in some
little village? Especially in a dull place like Kipworth?"

Not waiting for a reply to his questions, he continued. "I could understand it, perhaps, if it was hunting season; for I understand Dunford's father was an
avid member of the Quorn, with his own pack and
a stable full of exceptional mounts, but—"

"Freddy, I know what I saw. And I tell you, you
have not arrived a minute too soon."

"But even if you are right, my pet, what has any
of it to do with me?"

The gentleman's beloved rolled her eyes heavenward. "When was the last time you saw your niece?"

"Anna?"

With a sigh of resignation, she asked, "Have you
another one?"

"Not that I know of," he replied affably. "But what
has Anna to do with—"

"She is here. At this very inn. She and Sir Miles,
and their cousin, Miss Wilson."

"Harriet here? With the children?"

"A child Sir Miles may be, but I assure you the·

term can no longer be applied to Miss Anna Gwynn, who is certainly out of the schoolroom by now. Not to mention being as beautiful a young lady as I have ever clapped eyes on."

"Always was a pretty little thing. Even so, my love, what has this to say to Lord Dunford being in the neighborhood?"

"Earlier, Freddy, I saw your niece and nephew, along with Miss Wilson, leave the inn for an outing to the village."

"So? Nothing at all remarkable in that."

"Of course not. Not if they had been alone. As it happens, they were not. They left with an escort."

"As I said, nothing so very remarkable in—"

"Their escort was Lord Dunford himself."

"Dunford! Stap my vitals! Are you certain of this?"

"You need have no doubts as to the accuracy of my eyesight."

Never one to come to conclusions speedily, the gentleman mulled over all he had been told. After a full three minutes of strenuous concentration, he said, "Are you telling me that you suspect Lord Dunford of having come here in pursuit of my niece?"

His informant nodded. "As you remarked earlier, my dear, his lordship is never seen away from Town, and the hunting season has yet to begin. Add to that the fact that Miss Gwynn was at the inn for no more than a day before his lordship put in an appearance, and you can draw but one conclusion."

Convinced at last, Frederick Gwynn blessed himself. "Our little Anna and Lord Dunford. By Jove! What good luck!"

"Luck? Freddy, how can you even think it? Your niece is an innocent girl, while the man is known as Lord Care-For-Naught."

"But he is as rich as Golden Ball! The chit's got no dowry to speak of, and—"

"Even so, Dunford is—" She was obliged to bite off whatever comment she had hoped to make, for at just that moment the young lady under discussion descended the stairs and spied her guardian.

"Uncle Freddy!"

At sight of the beauty in the pale blue sarcenet dinner dress, Frederick Gwynn stood, his mouth agape. "Good God, Eunice! Never tell me this is my little Anna."

Such confirmation was unnecessary, for the young lady flew to her relative and threw her arms about his neck. While she embraced him, he looked over at the heiress, whose expression said, "I told you so."

"Stap me!"

Later, when Mr. Gwynn and Miss Shaw were once again alone, the gentleman was obliged to admit the truth of what he had been told. "You were in the right of it, Eunice. There can be no doubt that Lord Dunford has come here in pursuit of our Anna."

"As to my being right, I vow I take no delight in the fact. After all, with a man of Dunford's reputation, one must wonder if his intentions are honorable, or if he hopes to give the girl a slip on the shoulder."

"A slip on—But Anna is a lady! Dunford must know that."

"And what if he knows it, but he does not care?" Coming at last to her major reason for embracing the subject with such tenacity, the heiress said, "If that is the case, then what do you mean to do about it?"

"Do? I, er . . ." Unaccustomed to having to *do* anything where his niece and nephew were concerned, he looked to Miss Shaw for guidance.

"I expect," she said, as if the thought had come from his head and not her own, "that you will do what any man of sense would do. You will remain here to see that nothing untoward happens."

After a few moments of quiet contemplation, he said, "But what of your father? I sent him a letter asking if I might speak with him on a personal matter, and he will be expecting me by tomorrow at the latest."

"As to that, my dear Freddy, you can post another letter. Under the circumstances, my father will understand that your own family obligations must come first."

"So you are saying that I should delay my journey northward?"

Miss Shaw lowered her gaze lest he see the glow of success reflected in her eyes. "You must, of course, be guided by your own conscience. If I were to venture an opinion, however, I would say that for you to leave now would be a dereliction of your duty as Miss Gwynn's legal guardian and as acting head of your family."

"Oh, I say. Acting head of the—I never thought of it in that way." Resembling a peacock who has only just discovered his glorious tail feathers, Frederick Gwynn could not sit still, but stood and strolled around the room. Finally, coming back to the fireplace, he reclaimed his seat.

"Well? What is your decision?"

"It is as you said, my pet. I cannot in good conscience abandon my niece with only her cousin to look out for her. Females, you know. They always look to us males for guidance."

"As you say, Freddy."

While he basked in the glow of this new picture of himself as a man to whom others turned for leadership, the heiress proffered her next suggestion. "If you are decided upon this course of action, my dear, and I can only applaud you for your dedication to familial duty, perhaps you might wish to pay off your hired chaise. Later, when things are settled, we can continue to my home in the comfort of my private carriage."

More than happy to release his poorly sprung

hired conveyance in favor of one that would be infinitely more comfortable and would cost him not so much as a groat in expenses, he called for the innkeeper. "Shimmerhorn!"

"Yes, sir, Mr. Gwynn."

"I'll not be continuing my journey today." He tossed the man a small pouch of coins. "Pay the coachman, there's a good fellow, then see to my traps. And when you return, bring a bottle of your best Madeira."

"Right away, sir."

Satisfied that the essentials were taken care of, the gentleman stretched his highly polished, Hoby-made boots toward the fire. "Good thing you happened to be at this particular inn, my pet. Otherwise, I might have continued north, none the wiser regarding Lord Dunford's pursuit of my niece."

"As you say, it was fortunate that I decided to break my journey at just this spot. Meanwhile, this is an excellent opportunity for me to become better acquainted with your family."

"Capital idea. If I must stay here in Kipworth to look out for dear little Anna's interests, it will be pleasant to have you nearby."

"And why?" asked Harriet, who had descended the staircase in time to hear the gentleman's final comment, "the sudden concern for Anna's interests?"

Though the gentleman stood once again, this time he was not obliged to suffer an onslaught of hugs. Instead, Harriet merely shook his hand.

Frederick, having forgotten the forcefulness of the young woman's personality, suddenly felt on unsteady ground. "It is, er, all due to Lord Dunford."

"Lord Dunford? And what, pray, has he to do with Anna?"

"Everything, I should think, for his lordship is dangling after my niece."

"Of all the—" As if recalling to whom she spoke,

she bit back whatever she had meant to say. "If I may ask, Frederick, how came you by such a notion?"

Not at all pleased to have his thought processes questioned by one whom he had pictured earlier as being appreciative of his guidance, he spoke belligerently. "That need not concern you. Though, I assure you, my sources are unimpeachable. And . . . And as acting head of the family, it is my duty to remain in Kipworth until I see the fellow's betrothal ring on her finger."

Chapter Eight

Until I see his betrothal ring on her finger.
    The phrase sounded oddly familiar, and Harriet had no difficulty in guessing from whose lips it had originally sprung. As if to confirm the suspicion, she turned toward Miss Shaw, who gave her look for look, all but daring her to reveal the particulars of their earlier conversation.

"I am persuaded, Miss Wilson, that all will be well. You and your charges need not cut short your holiday, and in the meantime, Mr. Gwynn can take advantage of this excellent opportunity to spend a few days in company with his family. Surely you can find no fault with such a plan."

"No," Harriet agreed, "no fault whatsoever."

At least Frederick had not taken it into his head to ship Miles and Anna back to London on the instant. And though Harriet was happy with that development, she was not pleased when, following the evening meal, the gentleman invited her for a private chat. Unable to avoid the tête à tête, she walked with him to the horse chestnut tree that all but filled the side yard of the inn. She had no more than taken a seat on the rustic wooden bench when he took her to task for not being more watchful over his niece.

"I assure you," she said, not for the first time, "that Lord Dunford has not come anywhere near Anna."

"That is not the way I heard it. And to own the truth, Harriet, I am surprised at your laxness. One would expect a woman of your years to have better sense than to allow a man of Dunford's reputation near an impressionable girl."

A woman of your years!

Harriet bit her lip to still the angry reply that threatened to explode from within her. Truth to tell, she did not know which made her angrier, that a man at least sixteen years her senior should refer to her age as though she were practically in her dotage, or that a man with half her intelligence should question her judgment.

Whatever the primary cause, she was obliged to take a deep breath, then count backward from ten to keep from venting her ire. "As I explained before, Frederick, one of the gentlemen who accompanied us on our visit to St. Agnes's Church was, in fact, his lordship's younger brother, Mr. Burton Dunford. For that reason, it is possible that your informant mistook one brother for the other. Never having met his lordship myself, I cannot attest to their familial resemblance. I can assure you, however, that the other gentleman was not Lord Dunford."

All but ignoring her entire explanation, Frederick surprised her by remarking that it would be a splendid match. "A chit with her looks and a man with his wealth. What could be more felicitous?"

"Some might say a *tendre* for one another would be desirable."

"*Tendres.* Bah! You've been reading too much poetry, my girl. Take it from one who knows, *tendres*, like ices, never last."

Recalling that Frederick Gwynn was at that moment on his way to ask for the hand of a lady whose inheritance was her principal attraction, Harriet chose not to comment. Instead, hoping to put a period to the conversation, she suggested that he might find it enjoyable to join them on their outing the next day. "You could meet Mr. Randolph, thereby setting your mind at ease. I am persuaded that our host would not object to another gentleman in the party."

Knowing full well that Frederick Gwynn was purse pinched, she derived a certain amount of pleasure from adding, "Of course, you would have to hire a conveyance of some sort, for the landau will not hold more than four comfortably."

Since the prospect of further expenditures turned the gentleman's countenance quite pale, Harriet smiled sweetly, satisfied at having retaliated just a bit for his remark about her age. Deciding she had toyed with him long enough, she accepted his excuse that fatigue from his two days' travel would prompt him to remain abed until at least midday. "Good night, then, Frederick. And pray allow me to wish you pleasant dreams."

Rand, unaware that he had just escaped a face-to-face confrontation with Mr. Frederick Gwynn, a man who would recognize him on sight, finished his own evening meal, then strolled down toward the kennels. He needed some quiet time, for he was still concerned over the matter of the bullet that just missed hitting him.

Naturally, the yipping of the hounds announced his approach, and before he reached the fenced runs, Eli Porter unlatched the gate and stepped out.

"A good evening to yer lordship," the gnomelike little man said.

"You here at this hour, Eli?"

"Aye. Lida, one of the bitches, dropped a trio of whelps week 'fore last."

"And you had to assure yourself that all was well."

The old man cackled. "Ye know me too well, Master Rand."

"Is anything amiss?"

The huntsman shook his grizzled head. "Not with Lida. She be one of the good mothers. Give her life for her pups, she would. I were just having a look at 'em. Just for the pleasure of seeing the little ones sleeping peaceful-like, snuggled up to their mam's warmth, with their little furry bellies full from suckling."

Not wanting to discuss what was actually on his mind, Rand said, "And I was just having a look at the moon. I had forgotten how it hides behind the clouds this time of year, then suddenly bursts free, washing the trees and the land in palest gold."

"It does, and that's a fact." After several moments of silence, in which both men stared at the play of light upon the land, Eli said, "They didn't have no moon down in Barbados?"

"Not one I would ever care to see again."

The wizened old huntsman fell into step with Rand, and the two of them strolled along together for some time in silence, much as they had done years ago, when Rand was a lad no taller than Eli. As he had all those years ago, Eli said what was on his mind. "Lida's the best sort of mother. For most, it just seems to come natural. Knowing how to do for their pups. 'Course, sometimes there be one or two that have to be shown the way with the first litter. Second time around, though, they be just fine."

He hesitated for a moment, but Rand knew from experience that there was still something the old man wanted to say. He was just considering how best to say it.

"We had this one bitch once, 'bout ten years back, dropped her litters natural enough, but she didn't never seem to get the hang of taking care of 'em. Strange that. Never could get my nous box around it. I guess it just weren't in her. Couldn't teach her to care for them pups no more than I could change her eyes to blue."

Rand felt the peace of the evening shatter. He knew, somehow, that Eli was about to speak of the unspeakable, yet he was unable to say him nay.

"It were a heartless thing his lordship done, Master Rand, sending ye away like that. And it's been a heavy load on my conscience."

"Your conscience? But why?"

" 'Cause I knew how he was, and I should've looked out for ye."

"Eli, no. You were not to blame."

The old man pulled a bandanna from the sleeve of his smock and blew his nose. "His lordship were a hard man. Never give nothing a second chance. I knew that. Why, if a hound lost the scent, just once, his lordship'd say, 'Take 'im back to the kennel, Eli, and shoot 'im.' "

The old fellow cleared his throat, as if the memory still rankled. "Just like that, he'd say, 'Shoot 'im.' Seemed like a thing or a body had to be perfect, or his lordship didn't want it around."

"People are seldom perfect," Rand said.

"That be true enough. But ye were a good lad, and ye should've been given a second chance. Not that I believed you had aught to do with the daughter of that scoundrel Jem Coombs. Though Belle were a comely lass, ye were always too particular in yer ways to fancy the likes of her."

"You believed me?"

"Aye. But then, I knew ye."

Rand had trouble drawing breath into his lungs. *But then, I knew ye.* He could not believe the effect that one simple sentence had upon him.

As a child, he had looked up to the little man, realizing that in spite of the huntsman's size, he was a man worthy of respect. And now, to discover that Eli had believed in his innocence all along, had trusted him when his own father had readily believed the worst, was a gift more precious than he could say.

Apparently Eli did not expect a reply, so they continued in companionable silence for a time, until their walk brought them back to the stables, where Eli and the grooms occupied the loft rooms. Just before Rand bid the old huntsman a good night, Eli bent his head back so he could look up at the lad who had grown so tall. "His lordship didn't have ye shot, Master Rand, so I'm thinking there still be hope for ye. Let go yer anger, lad, and open yer heart while ye still can. Give yerself a second chance."

Eli's words were still playing inside Rand's head when he returned to the house. While he climbed the stairs, intent on seeking his bed and making an early night of it, he met Burton coming down. His brother merely nodded, clearly meaning to avoid any conversation, but Rand, thinking this was as good a place as any to begin that second chance, bid him wait up a moment.

"What do you want?" Burton asked, his tone not at all promising.

"Only this. To tell you that I am here for you should you need me."

"And why should I have need of you?"

"I went to Oxford before I came here," Rand said, "so I know about the Wexham brothers and their attempt to extort money from you."

"Damn you! Debauchery must have addled your brains. Otherwise, you would understand me when I tell you that I do not wish you meddling in my affairs."

Debauchery!

Curbing his disappointment at this poor start, Rand managed to speak quietly. "My transgressions aside, Burton, I understand you well enough. Believe it or not, we are more alike than you might wish to admit. I have been where you are now. I once was a young man with little experience of the world, no money to soften the harsh realities of life, and no family to support me in time of trouble. And, it may please you to know, I have taken more than a few beatings from the likes of the Wexhams."

The younger man made no reply. He merely stood like a statue, staring at a rather gory hunting scene hanging near the bottom of the staircase, his obvious purpose to refrain from showing the smallest interest in what his brother had to say. After a long silence, he said, "Are you finished?"

"Not quite, you young fool. I want you to know, as I did not, that you have a family to whom you can turn. You have me. I am your brother, and though you clearly wish me anyplace but here, I intend to stick to you like a nettle, at least until I am certain those three ruffians are no longer a threat."

"And if I do not wish your, er, nettlesome company?"

Rand smiled, as much at his brother's spunk as at the pun he had made. "Regrettably, your wishes have little to say to the matter. I am here, and here I stay."

"Go to hell!"

"That is, quite possibly, my ultimate destination. However—"

Whatever he had meant to say, the words remained unspoken, for Burton hurried down the stairs, taking them two at a time. Ignoring the footman who stood nearby, attempting to imitate a post, the angry young man yanked open the door, letting it slam against the wall. Then, without a backward glance, he ran out into the night.

After a time, Rand turned and continued up the stairs. He was still muttering to himself when he reached the master bedchamber. "You made a splendid mess of that, old boy."

"I beg your pardon?" his startled valet said.

Wanting to be left alone, he waved the servant away, then pulled out the leather-covered chair that matched the scarred old kneehole desk. After tearing up the letter he had written earlier, he found quill, ink, and writing paper, and penned a second letter to his man of business in London. As before, he instructed the man to send him the latest report from the Bow Street Runners regarding the Frenchman.

Though he was convinced that de la Croix was behind the attempted shooting, there was a slim chance that the target was not Rand but Burton. For that reason, he added a final paragraph, asking that another runner be hired and sent to Oxford to check on the whereabouts of the three Wexham brothers.

When the missive was finished and the plain, burgundy-colored wafer attached, Rand stretched out on the heavily carved tester bed, his hands behind his head, and reflected upon everything Eli Porter had said to him that evening. Unfortunately, his musings ended with his recollection of the confrontation with Burton on the stairs.

So much for his second chance at being a big brother. With every attempt at reconciliation, Burton despised him more. And why should he not? What did Rand know of brotherly love? Unlike Lida, who knew instinctively how to shield and nurture her new pups, he was no natural at this protective business. Obviously, he was one of those dogs who needed to be shown the way.

The next day, Rand woke with renewed hope. He had not felt this good in years, as if he were in complete charge of his destiny. Eli had bid him give himself a second chance, and he meant to take the little huntman's advice.

Dressed in his newest coat, an ocher color that complemented his nut-brown breeches and top boots, and whistling slightly off-key, he climbed aboard the freshly washed and polished landau. Without a word, Burton fell in behind the carriage, riding a handsome gray from the stables. It was obvious he meant to accompany them to Bosworth Field, and equally obvious that he did not mean to exchange pleasantries with his older brother, not while they were alone, in any event.

So be it! For now, at least. Rand had dealt with far stubborner people. Let Burton give him the silent treatment. Nothing could dampen Rand's enthusiasm for the day ahead—a day he would spend in the company of the most delightful lady he had ever met.

No, Harriet Wilson was more than delightful. She was smart, she was honest, and she was kind—traits Rand had seen little of in his lifetime—and she had done him the honor of calling him her friend.

Of course, to enjoy the lady's company, he must include her two young cousins, but that was no great sacrifice. Miles Gwynn and his sister were thoroughly likeable, and it gave Rand pleasure to show them a bit of the countryside. For a man known as Lord Care-For-Naught, perhaps enjoying giving someone else pleasure was the beginning of that second chance.

Miles, whose cousin had said he was army mad, had obviously been waiting in the inn yard for some time for the day's outing to begin. The coachman had only just halted the well-matched pair hitched to the landau, and Rand was preparing to step down, when the lad ran out of the Rose and Crown and stood beside the carriage, impatiently shifting his weight from one foot to the other. "Mr. Randolph," he said, touching the bill of his cap. "Good day to you, sir. I am ready to go."

"So I see, my boy. In fact," he added, schooling

his face so he did not reveal his amusement at the lad's exuberance, "it would appear that you are a person who understands the virtue of punctuality. An admirable trait, to be sure. Unfortunately, since I have found it to be primarily a masculine attribute, and not one generally embraced by ladies, I fear we must wait for your sister and Miss Wil—"

"For that slur on womankind," Harriet said from the doorway, "it would serve you right, sir, if Anna and I returned to our bedchambers and left you to cool your heels for at least half an hour."

Because she was smiling, and was even then opening a pretty willow-green parasol against the sun's rays, Rand did not take the threat seriously. Instead, he strolled over to the door, offered her his arm, then complimented her on the acuteness of her hearing. "I see I shall have to learn to speak more softly."

"That, sir, or else learn to sweeten your words. After all, you never know when you will be obliged to eat them."

He laughed aloud. "Like now, for instance?"

For her answer, she looked over her shoulder at her lovely cousin, who was even then emerging from the rustic building, a picture of youthful beauty beneath a primrose parasol fashioned of gathered silk and tiny bows. "Ah, Anna," she said, "as always, you are right on time."

At the young lady's raised eyebrows, Harriet informed her that Mr. Randolph appreciated punctuality. "One might even say he finds punctuality delicious."

"Viper," he said, the whispered word just loud enough for her to hear.

Her laughing response was low and delightfully throaty, and when she made no attempt to hide her amusement, Rand was obliged to conquer an almost overwhelming desire to take her in his arms and cover those smiling lips with his own. He did nothing of the kind, of course; instead, he merely put his hand beneath her elbow and assisted her into the carriage.

"Miss Gwynn," Burton said, hurrying forward to offer the young lady his hand. "What a pretty parasol. I shall never see yellow again without thinking of it as your color."

"I like Cousin Harriet's parasol," Miles said, almost as if he thought she was being slighted. "She has had it forever, of course, but green is my favorite color."

The lady with the ancient accoutrement leaned forward and gave the boy's cap a playful tug that pulled it down over his eyes. "I can always depend upon you, Miles, to lift my spirits."

Everyone laughed, and as if suddenly remembering his manners, Burton bowed to Harriet. "Whatever the age of the parasol, ma'am, it is a pretty shade for a pretty lady."

"Why, thank you, Mr. Dunford. And while we are passing around compliments, allow me to comment on that very handsome gray. Your stable must be extensive, for I do not think you rode that same animal yesterday."

"Since the stables, like the horses in them, belong to my brother, you must address your compliments to him."

"When you meet him," Rand said.

After giving Burton a none-too-gentle shove toward the gray under discussion, Rand took his seat beside Miles in the landau and gave the coachman the office to drive on.

"Bosworth Field," Miles said, elated to be on his way at last, "here we come."

More than an hour later, when the landau passed through Market Bosworth, then traveled southward for about two miles, Miles began looking all about

him for signs of the battle site. Finding none, he
asked if they were nearly there.

"Miles!" his sister cautioned. "Remember your
manners."

"Beg pardon, sir."

"Not at all, my boy. It is a fair question; for if I
remember correctly, the field is not posted. Not the
first sign to honor its significance."

For the last quarter of an hour, they had driven
past stretches of hedge and small woods that were
there as a result of fox-hunting farmers—farmers
who were more interested in providing living quar-
ters for the fox than with preserving the site of the
battle that had ended the Wars of the Roses. Rand
understood this; after all, that series of wars had
dragged on for a century, and they had occurred more
than three hundred years ago. Farmers were obliged
to live in the present, and for the inhabitants of Leicestershire, a prosperous present meant hunting.

When the landau arrived at a bit of high ground
known as Ambien Hill, Rand bid the coachman stop
the team. "There," he said to Miles, stretching out
his hand as if offering the lad the acres and acres of
rolling green land and scattered trees. "Before you
lies Bosworth Field."

The field had a hushed quality about it, with little
disturbing the silence save the mournful *coo coo coo*
of a morning dove in the distance, and the chattering
of a pair of red squirrels in one of the ancient spread-
ing oaks in the foreground.

It was too much to hope that the excited ten-year-
old would respect the peace of the landscape, and he
all but tumbled out of the carriage, with Rand alight-
ing at a more leisurely pace, then turning to offer
his hand to the ladies. Within moments, Burton had
dismounted and joined them, hurrying to offer Anna
his arm for the walk across the uneven ground.

"From here," Rand said, addressing his remark to an awed Miles, "we will descend the hill, thereby following the route taken by Richard the Third and his men on that fateful day in 1485."

"All ten thousand of them," the boy added, as if to show their host that he was not completely uniformed.

"Right you are, lad. Accompanying the king were several prominent lords, knights, esquires, and an enormous throng of common people, many of them tenants of the lords."

"A formidable army," the boy added, "marching against Henry Tudor's troops, which numbered scarcely five thousand."

Harriet, who had accepted Rand's arm, was not surprised at her young cousin's ability to supply pertinent facts about the battle, but she feigned astonishment at their host's knowledge. "What an interesting display of information, Mr. Randolph. One might almost suppose that you had consulted a guidebook prior to making the journey."

He laughed. "I am found out. Are you disappointed, ma'am? Were you in hopes of proving me a humbug once again?"

"Not at all, sir. In truth, you find me almost as fascinated as Miles. Therefore, if you have information at hand, pray, let nothing I have said on past occasions deter you from imparting it."

Happy to comply with her request, he raised his voice so that Anna and Burton could hear as well. "Imagine, if you will, the king's men-at-arms in the lead, brandishing battle-ax, mace, and flail, and with their egg-shaped helmets and their plated armor offering little target for Henry's bowmen. To right and left, Richard's bowmen move forward, their soft tunics, which reached down to their thighs, allowing them to move quickly in the August heat."

"August?" Anna asked. "Then the weather must have been quite like today. Sunny and warm."

"Right you are," Burton said, gazing at the young lady in the adoring manner that put his brother in mind of a Bedlamite. "Unfortunately, the king's soldiers were not so fortunate as to possess parasols."

If the look of disgust on Miles's face was anything to go by, he did not appreciate a return to the subject of feminine *fol lols*. "After the archers," he said, addressing his remarks solely to Harriet and their host, "came the swordsmen, their weapon in one hand, while with the other hand they held their iron shield in front of them."

Playing to the boy's enthusiasm, Rand spoke softly at first, as he had heard actors do on the stage when they wished to add a note of drama. "Finally," he said, "Richard's men, advancing to attack in the traditional wedge formation, met Henry's vanguard." After pausing an instant for dramatic effect, Rand gradually increased his volume. "The moment of truth had come at last, and a fierce battle ensued."

"Charge!" Miles yelled.

As if taking part in that battle, the boy ran downward toward a stretch of flattish land, all the while brandishing an imaginary sword and occasionally instructing an equally imaginary foe to "Take that, you blackguard!"

As for Harriet and Rand, they followed in the lad's wake, enjoying his enthusiasm, though they were never certain for whom he fought, the king or the usurper.

"Sir," she said, "you missed your calling. You should have gone on the stage. I am persuaded the hairs are still standing on the back of my neck."

Rand knew she was teasing, so he felt free to peer beneath the parasol as if to check for himself the validity of her remark. From what he could see of her neck, it was lovely as a swan's, the skin soft and satiny, without the first signs of gooseflesh.

It was a neck meant for stroking. For kissing. And for just a moment he let himself imagine a scene in which her long, thick tresses fell freely about her shoulders. She would be smiling up at him, and he would slip his hand beneath those tresses to cup her neck, then bend his head to meet hers, their lips—

"Charge!" Miles yelled again, bringing the gentleman's thoughts, if not his throbbing pulses, back to the present.

Apparently, the lady had not been caught up in visions of Rand caressing her neck, and as if suddenly mindful of where she stepped, she looked down at the ground beneath her half boots. Slowly she lifted her troubled, pansy eyes to his. "Please tell me, sir, that I am not treading on soil once reddened by the blood of slain soldiers."

"Who can say?" Lowering his voice, he added, "This might, in fact, be the wrong spot entirely."

"What! Why, Mr. Randolph, I had thought you a man of honor. And now, to my dismay, I discover that you are given to deception."

For just a moment, Rand felt as if his cravat might choke him. The lady was teasing him again, of course, but what would she say later, when she discovered that he was deceiving her by letting her believe he was a plain mister? Not wishing to spoil this pleasurable outing by contemplating his eventual discovery, he put his finger across his lips to signal for her silence. "Shh. Would you have yonder soldier hear you?"

"Not for the world," she said, placing a finger across her own lips.

"That is what I thought. Let us agree, then, to be coconspirators. Unless, of course, you are wishful of returning to the carriage and searching out another battlefield entirely?"

The quick shake of her head gave him his answer.

She gave his arm a tug, so he would lean down, allowing her to whisper her next question. With her lips only inches from his ear, Rand breathed in the soft, clean, lemony fragrance of her skin.

Heaven help him! She smelled wonderful. And all Rand could think of was how easy it would be to turn his head just that little bit and taste her oh-so-tempting lips.

Unaware that she was testing the limits of his endurance, the lady whispered quite innocently, "Where is the actual field?" For a moment, Rand could not answer, for the feel of her warm breath had awakened inside him an entire plethora of unlooked-for emotions.

Finally, after running a finger inside the collar of his shirt to ease the pressure on his throat, he was able to answer her question. "As it happens, ma'am, though the meeting at Bosworth Field proved to be the decisive battle between the houses of York and Lancaster, putting an end to the Plantagenet line and marking the beginning of the Tudor reign, the historians of the day wrote almost nothing about it."

"Oh," she said.

Unfortunately, that single word necessitated a pursing of her lips, a circumstance that obliged Rand to employ all his resolve to keep his thoughts on the ancient battle, and not the battle presently being waged inside him.

"In truth," he said, swallowing to banish the husky note that had crept into his voice, "so little was actually recorded about the site that it is not even possible to draw an accurate map. All that is known for certain is that the fighting took place, that it was in this general area, and that Richard's horse became mired in a low-lying damp spot—some say it was a marsh. And, of course, that Richard was subsequently slain."

As if on cue, Miles, having given up his career as a swordsman to take on the persona of the king himself, dropped to his knees, as if grievously injured. While holding his side, in an attempt to stanch supposed blood flowing from a supposed wound, he cried out, "A horse, a horse. My kingdom for a horse!"

When no loyal subject came forward with a replacement animal, the lad fell backward upon the ground, his arms spread wide. With his final, gasping breath, he called out, "I am killed. Farewell, England. Farewell."

Chapter Nine

They remained at Bosworth Field a good two hours, a span of time roughly equal to that of the actual battle; then the party retired to the nearby village of Wigby, and the White Owl Inn. The owner of the neat, yet unprepossessing establishment was pleased to greet so distinguished a party, and he voiced his pleasure at being able to supply the ladies with a private room for their convenience.

Within a matter of minutes, their ablutions made, and their parasols, reticules, bonnets, and gloves left on the bed, Harriet and Anne joined the gentlemen in the small dining parlor. After a morning spent walking across acres of rough land, Harriet was more than agreeable to taking her place at the round, cloth-draped table, where a pot of aromatic tea steeped beneath a colorful, petit-point cozy. Following the first reviving sips of the steaming brew, Harriet declared herself content. "For my part, should the innkeeper serve us nothing save cold turnips and stale bread, he would hear no complaint from me."

"Turnips!" young Miles said, his face a study of revulsion. "Cousin, you know I cannot abide that nasty vegetable."

As it happened, the boy was in luck, for not a single root vegetable was brought to the table. Furthermore, the palatableness of the nuncheon far surpassed all their expectations. They were served a delicious fillet of sole in a white wine sauce with mushrooms, accompanied by a vegetable pie whose crust was so flaky it practically melted in the mouth, and a blancmange whipped to perfection then filled with a combination of toasted almonds, sugared raisins, and apricot preserves.

A good hour later, with scarcely a crumb remaining, Miles finished the last of the dessert—his third serving—then licked the sugar from his fingers. "I vow," he said, "I shall never eat again."

"Now that," replied his sister, "is something I should like to see. Especially when you seem bent upon eating our poor cousin out of house and home."

"I am doing no such thing. Am I, Cousin Harriet?"

"Of course not," the lady replied. "When last I looked, the rear of the house still stood."

At the lad's indignant humph, everyone laughed.

"Headed for the poorhouse, are you?" Rand asked.

She shook her head. "Not today, in any event. But if I were, it would not be the result of feeding one admittedly grubby ten-year-old boy."

"Thank you," said the lad. After scraping back his chair and standing, he showed his appreciation to his benefactress by snatching a spoonful of half-eaten blancmange reposing on her plate and popping it into his mouth.

Rand and Burton stared in surprise at such behavior, but the lady merely laughed. "Lucky for you, Miles Gwynn, that I had put down my fork. Otherwise, King Richard's wound would have been nothing to those inflicted upon you."

Miss Gwynn sighed. "Mr. Randolph, Mr. Dunford, you must know that my cousin is forever promising dire consequences. Unfortunately, she never carries through on her threats, and as a result, my brother is quite incorrigible."

Harriet Wilson winked at the lad, who had placed his arm around her shoulders and was leaning against her side. "I am turning over a new leaf," she said. "So be warned, you incorrigible mudlark, for next time I shall certainly give you what for."

The threat was obviously worn smooth by repetition, for Miss Gwynn rolled her eyes heavenward. "That, too, is something I should like to see."

The brothers exchanged glances, for never in their lives had they sat at table with a family who were more relaxed and unaffected.

"Pray, forgive our foolishness," Harriet said, giving the boy a squeeze, then gently pushing him aside and bidding him take his seat until everyone was finished. "You gentlemen will be thinking that my cousins and I are totally devoid of manners."

"Not at all," Burton said.

"Actually," Rand added, almost as if thinking aloud, "I was wondering, ma'am, if your middle name might be Lida."

"Who is Lida?" Anna asked some time later, when she and Harriet returned to the private bedchamber to freshen up and reclaim their bonnets and parasols.

"I have no idea."

"How odd, then, that Mr. Randolph should think it a part of your name."

While the young lady placed the small, chip-straw bonnet on her fair curls and tied the ribbons beneath her chin, she studied Harriet in the looking glass. "I hope you will forgive me for saying this, Cousin, but . . ."

"But what?"

"It is just that there are a number of things about Mr. Randolph that I do not understand."

"Oh?" Harriet said, far too nonchalantly. "Pray, what might those be?"

"For one thing, I remember that you said you and

he had met several months ago, but you never mentioned any of the particulars. How you met, for example. Or where."

"Did I not?"

"You know you did not. And judging by your evasiveness, it would appear that I am to be none the wiser for having introduced the subject."

When Harriet made no reply, Anna continued. "He is a gentleman, anyone can see that, and none but the highest sticklers would fault his easy manners and address. However, I cannot quite rid myself of the feeling that there is some important fact he is keeping to himself. Do you not sense something a bit mysterious about him?"

"Mysterious? Why? Because he once lived in Barbados? Anna, my dear, those pirate stories he told Miles were pure make-believe. I beg you not to allow your imagination to get the better of you."

"I . . . I do not think I have done so."

"You must have, my dear, if you think there is anything amiss about Mr. Randolph."

Anna looked down at her hands, embarrassed, but taking the reproof without rancor. "I know I am young," she said quietly, "and I have nothing like your experience before the world, but I do not consider mine a fanciful nature. And, of course, I will gladly admit to being foolish if you will tell me, Cousin, that you know who he is. Or even where he lives."

"I, uh . . ."

When she hesitated, Anna said, "Aside from his being a guest at Lord Dunford's hunting box, has he mentioned other of his friends? His family?"

Harriet shook her head, not at all pleased with this line of questioning. "He has mentioned no one. Nor have I asked, for I am loath to pry into his personal affairs." Turning the tables, she said, "Have you asked after Mr. Dunford's friends?"

"No. But there is no reason why I should. I am not smitten with Mr. Dunford. Nor am I likely to be; for my mother, God rest her soul, had her heart set on my having a successful come-out, and I have determined to do nothing to interfere with her plans."

Hearing nothing beyond the word "smitten," Harriet felt her face grow warm. "I assured you, Anna, that I am not smitten with Mr. Randolph."

The younger lady was silent for some time, as if forming her next remarks. "I hope you know, Cousin, that I both love and admire you, and not for the world would I have you think me impertinent, or that this conversation is a result of mere idle curiosity. Believe me, nothing could be further from the truth."

"Of course not."

"Your happiness," she continued, "is of primary importance to me, and not simply because Miles and I make our home with you. That is, however, one of my concerns. And in the interest of mine and Miles's future living arrangements, I feel I must ask if you have a *tendre* for Mr. Randolph."

"A *tendre!* My dear, I barely know the gentleman."

"And what has that to say to the point?"

"A great deal, I should think."

"Not," Anna said, "if you love him."

"Which, I promise you, I do not."

Apparently unwilling to accept her cousin's protestations, Anna crossed the small bedchamber and caught Harriet's hands between her own. "And have you hopes of seeing your feelings returned?"

If Harriet's cheeks were warm before, now they were positively inflamed. The questions were legitimate, and no one had a better right to ask them than Anna, who was more like a sister to her than a cousin. And yet, the answers were not that simple. "I cannot tell you, my dear, because I do not know."

Unwilling to be put off, Anna said, "About which

part are you uncertain? That you have a *tendre* for the gentleman? Or that you hope to see your feelings returned?"

"Neither. Both. Oh, how can I say? Besides, it is I who should be asking these questions of you. Especially since your uncle would have it that you are being pursued by Mr. Burton Dunford's rather disreputable brother."

It was Anna's turn to look surprised. "Lord Dunford? Uncle Freddy thinks—" She laughed so hard she was obliged to hold her sides. "Now there is a good joke, indeed, for I have never even seen his lordship. All I know of him is what you have told me, Cousin, and believe me, nothing you have said has made me wish to pursue his acquaintance."

"Nor I," replied her cousin. "The last person in the world I should wish to know is Lord Dunford."

It was well past four of the clock when the coachman brought the landau around to the front of the White Owl. Rand had sent word to the driver to harness the team; then while he settled the bill with the innkeeper, the ladies had walked around to a small wildflower garden on the far side of the inn.

Later, when the business of the bill was completed, Rand ventured out to the garden. To his delight, Miles and Burton had taken themselves off someplace, and Miss Gwynn was some distance away, pursuing a bright yellow butterfly whose destination was a scarlet lady's slipper. That left her cousin standing quite alone near an apple tree whose immature fruit were still a bright green.

Happy to have a few moments alone with Miss Wilson, he removed his hat and made her an exaggerated bow. "May I hope, dear lady, that I do not interrupt fond memories of a certain donkey?"

The lady laughed. "Though you asked but one

question, sir, I am obliged to make my answer twofold. First, my memories of that beast are far from
fond, and second, you do not interrupt."

"That last part, at least, I am happy to hear, for I
have a favor I should like to ask of you."

The lady sighed as if much put-upon. "If that is
not just like the members of your sex! First you treat
me and my family to an absolutely marvelous outing;
then you compound the offense by arranging a wonderful nuncheon. Then, secure in the knowledge that
you have me under an obligation to you, you come
asking favors."

She sighed again. "I might have known how it
would be. What would you have me do, Mr. Randolph? Shall I slay a dragon? Write a sonnet? Or
perhaps you merely wish me to walk back to Kipworth so Mr. Dunford might ride in the landau?"

It was the gentleman's turn to laugh. "Nothing so
unchivalrous, I assure you. I meant only to ask if you
would be so good as to save me a dance tomorrow
evening. That is, if you mean to attend the assembly?"

For Harriet's part, nothing would please her more
than to dance with Mr. Randolph. She had not attended an assembly since before her father's death,
and she was captivated by the very thought of twirl-
ing about the room once again, as though she were
still a carefree girl. Of course, she was a girl no
longer, but she did not find that so very bad. Now
that she was a woman grown, if the musicians
should play a waltz, she could engage in that daring
dance without fear of censure.

The notion of waltzing with Mr. Randolph quite
stole the breath from her lungs. As well, her heart
raced at the very idea of their romantic embrace, for
her hand would be upon his broad shoulder, and his
hand would be at her waist, masterfully obliging her
to move in whatever direction he led.

As if reading her thoughts, he said, "Might they play a waltz, do you think?"

"I . . . I cannot say. In any event, I had not expected an assembly room in such a small village, and as a consequence, I brought no suitable gown."

Reading the disappointment in his gray eyes was very nearly enough to make Harriet willing to attend the affair in her night rail if necessary.

"As you say, ma'am, it is a small village. For that reason, I cannot think that anyone would judge you to be unsuitably attired in whatever dinner dress you brought with you."

Having lived her entire life in Town, Harriet was not conversant with the mode of dress acceptable in a place the size of Kipworth, but with her heart beating at such a rapid pace, she chose to believe the gentleman's assertion.

"If what you say is true, Mr. Randolph, then I shall be most happy to save you a dance."

"Thank you," he said softly. Then, catching her hand, he lifted her fingers to his lips, an act that put Harriet in mind of their first meeting, when he had pressed those lips against hers. It had been a magical kiss, and she had never forgotten it.

Apparently, the gentleman's thoughts were on much more serious matters, for he had grown rather quiet. "Is aught amiss?" she asked.

"From our very first meeting," he said, "that night you took me into your home and tended my wounds, I have asked myself what act of mine made me deserving of such good fortune. Meeting you has been the most positive experience of my life."

"It . . . it has?"

"Without question. Unfortunately, if I have learned anything during my rather checkered career, it is that a price must be paid for all things."

"A price? I do not understand, sir. I have asked nothing of you."

"Very true, ma'am, you have not. A fact that makes my position even more untenable. You have given me your friendship freely, and without reservation, and you will never know what that gift has meant to me."

He had not yet released her hand, and now he studied it, running his thumb over the ringless fingers. "The price to be paid is, I fear, mine. And the currency is honesty."

Harriet could not even guess what he wished to say to her, but from the seriousness of his expression, he obviously deemed it important. "Miss Wilson," he began, "there is something I must tell—"

"Is it time to leave?" Anna asked, surprising them both with her sudden appearance.

Rand was obliged to bite back an oath. His disappointment at the interruption must have shown on his face, for the young lady blushed, then asked his pardon. "It . . . It would appear that I have intruded on a private conversation."

She had, of course, for Rand had finally come to the conclusion that he must put an end to the lies and disclose his true identity. Miss Wilson deserved that much from him.

Naturally, what he needed to say required privacy; he could say none of it in front of Miss Gwynn. No more than he could cast aside good manners and tell the young lady that he wished she would take herself off. Find another butterfly to chase. Anything, just grant him and her cousin a few minutes alone.

Frustrated at having to postpone a confession he had found unbelievably difficult to broach, Rand answered her original question without thinking, saying the first thing that entered his head. "The landau is ready, Miss Gwynn, but we cannot leave without our missing brothers."

The instant the words left his mouth, Rand realized his mistake. The younger lady appeared to have found nothing unusual in his remark, but Harriet Wilson gave him a puzzled look. "I had no idea, Mr. Randolph, that you had a broth—"

"Please," he said softly, gazing so deeply into her eyes that Harriet could not have looked away had her life depended on it, "would you do me the honor of calling me Rand?"

The unexpected request caused a mad fluttering inside Harriet's chest, for to call a gentleman by his name, to display such familiarity before the world, would signify a very personal attachment indeed. He had been away from England for a dozen years; perhaps he did not realize the significance of his request. And yet, what if he did?

That very peculiar speech he had made about meeting her being the most positive experience of his life, and about everything having a price. Had that been his way of introducing another, more personal conversation? He had said he wanted to tell her something. Did he mean ask? Was he . . . Could he be wishful of making her an offer?

The very thought that he might wish to propose marriage sent Harriet's brain into a spin.

Scarcely half an hour ago, she had repudiated Anna's claim that she had a *tendre* for Mr. Randolph, or that she was in love with him. And yet, never before had Harriet experienced such delight in another person's company. Never before had the very presence of a gentleman made her feel as if the sky was bluer, the distant hills greener, and the air sweeter. Nor had her heart ever threatened to jump right out of her chest at the very sound of a man's voice, or her knees grow weak each time he smiled at her.

Could that be love?

From the first moment she met him, he had never completely left her thoughts. Six months ago he had figured as the most exciting man she had never known, and the time she had spent with him over the past few days had only reinforced that earlier assessment.

Could it be true then? Had she a *tendre* for Mr. Randolph? Was she in love with him.

The answer was, of course, a resounding, "Yes!"

The drive back to Kipworth was the most wonderful experience of Harriet's life. It was as if the landau had sprouted wings, and she was being borne on those wings—just she and the man she loved. She could think of nothing but the way he had kissed her fingers, and the fact that tomorrow evening he would dance with her, would hold her in his arms, and later, perhaps, search out a private spot where he might hold her even closer and kiss her eager lips.

"Do you not think so?" Anna asked, bringing Harriet down to earth for a moment.

"Of . . . Of course," she replied. She had not the least inkling what was being discussed, but her reply must have served, for no one turned to stare at her as though she were insane.

In truth, her senses were in a sort of whirlwind, so much so that under no circumstances could she have repeated even a single word of the conversation. Her ears were stopped to all voices save Rand's deep, rich baritone, just as her eyes were closed to all faces save his. He was so unbelievably handsome. And she was the luckiest woman in the world to have won the affection of such a man.

True, she knew little about him, but what did it matter where he lived and who were his friends? She knew the two most important facts, that he was an honorable man, and that she loved him with all her heart. She would have days, weeks, years to learn all those little insignificant facts. After all, she and Rand would have a lifetime together.

Rand. Just thinking of his name sent shivers down her spine.

Without her knowing it, the landau had arrived at the Rose and Crown, and as the coachman guided the matched pair into the inn yard, one of the ostlers ran from the stable to stand at the horses's heads. Miles leaped from the carriage first, then turned to offer his hand to his sister. Next, Rand stepped down and assisted Harriet. To her delight, he did not let go of her hand immediately, and while she marveled at how familiar his fingers felt already, and how strong yet sensitive they were, he used his other hand to fetch a coin for the ostler.

Mesmerized by every movement of his, Harriet watched while the man she loved pushed aside the lapels of his ocher-colored coat, revealing a beautifully tailored, cream-colored waistcoat. While he dug into one of the waistcoat pockets for the coin, Harriet noticed the handsomely embroidered ribbon dangling from his fob pocket.

He had impeccable taste. Understated, but elegant. Why, even the ribbon was—

She got no further, for her attention was caught by the gold fob attached to the end of the embroidered ribbon. It was a most unusual piece of jewelry—a peregrine falcon, perched on a leafless limb. The bird's eyes were two subtle beads of amber, and to duplicate the falcon's pale russet breast, the jeweler had introduced a hint of copper to the gold.

Harriet knew all about the addition of that hint of copper. She should, for she had been the one to add it. She was the jeweler who had create that particular falcon.

For a moment she could not breathe. She could not think. She had fashioned that fob for Lord Dunford, the most notorious libertine in London. How had it come to be in Mr. Randolph's possession?

While she watched silently, her brain unable to focus on any one thing, the gentleman found the coin, tossed it to the ostler, then turned to bid Harriet good-bye. "Thank you," he said, warmth in every word, "for a wonderful day."

He smiled at her then, only this time her knees did not go weak. Concentrating on those finely chiseled lips and those strong, white teeth, she recalled that she had once thought the man possessed the devil's own smile. How prophetic? How insightful?

Harriet bit her bottom lip to still its tremor, for in that instant she knew the truth. Knew it beyond a glimmer of doubt. There was no Mr. Randolph. There never had been. The man before her—the man smiling at her, charming her as only he knew how—was none other than Lord Care-For-Naught.

Chapter Ten

During the short drive from the Rose and Crown to the hunting box, Rand had spent the time composing a letter in his mind—a letter to Harriet Wilson explaining how he had come to misrepresent himself to her. In his entire life, he had never composed such an important document, had never felt instinctively that every word was significant, that each phrase should be chosen with care.

It was imperative that the lady receive the letter before tomorrow evening's assembly, for young Miles had mentioned that his Uncle Freddy was now staying at the inn. Though Frederick Gwynn was beef witted, under normal circumstances he was a harmless enough fellow; even so, he could do Rand a great deal of harm. Especially if he spoke with Harriet before she received the letter.

If Frederick Gwynn should inform the lady that her friend, Mr. Randolph, was none other than Lord Dunford, Harriet would never believe that Rand had not meant to deceive her. He must convince her of his sincerity, for she was his friend, and he could not bear the thought of losing her.

"Never," he muttered.

While the coachman reined in the pair, so that his passenger might alight beneath the shallow portico of the hunting box, Mr. Burton Dunford surrendered his horse to the groom, then remained beside the heavy walnut door, as if waiting for his brother. Though Rand would have liked a little more time to himself—time to continue his mental composition of the letter—he saw right away that Burton had something on his mind.

"Will you join me for a game of billiards?" Burton asked quietly, as though he made such a request on a daily basis.

Rand agreed, of course. This was the first olive branch his brother had extended, and he would let nothing stop him from accepting it. "Allow me to step above stairs for a moment. Then I will join you in, say, quarter of an hour?"

"Quarter of an hour," Burton agreed rather shyly, not making eye contact.

Within the appointed fifteen minutes, the two brothers were in the game room, their coats thrown over the back of a worn leather couch, and their shirt-sleeves rolled up to their elbows.

While they chose cues from the tall, polished walnut rack that was affixed to the wall nearest the billiards table, Rand asked his brother what was on his mind. To his amazement, his question did not meet with a rebuff.

"Can you remember," Burton asked, "how it was when you were a lad of Miles Gwynn's age?"

Rand chuckled. "I can. And though you may find this difficult to believe, to me it does not seem all that long ago. Why do you ask?"

His brother did not answer the question, but posed another. "When you were ten years old, were you ever at table with our mother?"

Rand was obliged to smother a scoff. "Surely you jest? Until I was old enough to attend Oxford, I was in our lady mother's presence only when accompanied by some servant who could whisk me away at a moment's notice. First the nursery maid, then the governess, and later my tutor. And at no time, no matter how exemplary my behavior, was I invited to partake of a meal. Not even a simple tea."

Burton said nothing more for a while, merely found the billiard balls and placed them on the baize-covered table. "I remember my early years as well," he said finally. "And though I have searched my brain, I cannot recall ever being at table with our mother. Never mind snatching a sweet from her plate.

"And," he added quietly, "though I was no grubbier than the typical lad of ten, I do not recall her ever putting her arm around me, or allowing me to put mine around her."

Though he turned his back to Rand, pretending an interest in the precise positioning of the billiard balls, Rand was not deceived, for he had heard the slight catch in his brother's voice. "You are thinking of our nuncheon," he said softly, "and of the obvious affection that exists between Miss Wilson, young Miles, and Miss Gwynn."

Burton nodded. "I never suspected that such interaction between adults and children took place. And had I ever imagined it, I could not have guessed that it would be tolerated by the adult. Nay, welcomed." A full minute went by before he spoke again. "What a lovely lady she is."

"Miss Gwynn?"

His brother seemed surprised by the question. "Miss Anna Gwynn is without a doubt the most beautiful creature I have ever beheld, but it was her cousin to whom I referred. Miss Wilson is a very special lady."

"Very true," Rand said, unable to stop the smile that tugged at his lips. "Miss Harriet Wilson is a pearl of great price."

Burton did not reply, and only after he had taken his first shot and missed, without coming anywhere close to the object ball, did he look at his brother again. "Rand?"

"Yes?"

"I had thought you interested in Miss Gwynn, but I believe I was mistaken. It is Miss Wilson who has caught your attention, is it not?"

"Anyone who knows Miss Wilson must admire her."

"Very true, but . . ." Burton cleared his throat, as if hesitant to continue. Finally, he said, "You do not mean the lady any harm, do you?"

Rand had already leaned across the table, preparing for his shot, but at the question he straightened. It was a fair question, and far from being angry with his brother for having asked it, he liked him all the better for it. "You have my solemn oath," he said, "that I will never cause the lady a moment's pain."

Harriet was numb with pain. She had no recollection of entering the inn, or of climbing the stairs. All she knew for certain was that she had finally reached her bedchamber where she could shut and lock the door.

After tossing her parasol, her bonnet, and her reticule onto the oak dressing table, she threw herself down on the bed and pulled one of the feather pillows over her face to muffle the sobs that would be denied no longer. She cried until the pillow was sodden with her tears. Then she cried some more. She did not even attempt to end the lachrymose orgy until her temples had begun to throb and the back of her head ached as though a band of spiteful elves had been at work with their little hammers, pounding away at her skull.

Of course, that pain was nothing when compared to the ache in her heart!

As she lay quietly, with her eyes closed and the anguish of her emotions like a vise wringing the life from her heart, she remembered something she had read in the guidebook Mr. Shimmerhorn kept near the inn door. The author of the book had extolled the wonders of the town of Leicester, which was but an afternoon's drive from Kipworth. The larger town, according to the writer, was the traditional home of the legendary King Lear and his three daughters.

"King Lear," Harriet muttered, recalling the old monarch and the daughters who had deceived him. "How appropriate."

Like the king, Harriet had been incredibly gullible. But unlike Lear, she did not have the excuse of old age and fatigue. She had fallen in love with a handsome face and a manly physique, not to mention a smile positively designed to beguile the foolish among her sex.

She had trusted him completely, and now she was left to wonder just how much of a fool she had been. Had her deceiver been less handsome, less charming, would she have been less naive?

She had thought they were friends. Yet how could there be friendship without honesty? He had told her he was Mr. Randolph, and she had believed him. She had *wanted* to believe him. Like one besotted, she had even convinced herself that he meant to ask her to be his wife.

Ha! The man was a libertine. Such men did not marry dowerless spinsters.

And yet, why that odd conversation in the wildflower garden? All that talk of *him* paying the price. If it was not a prelude to a proposal of marriage, then what was it?

She had no sooner asked herself the question than a horrible suspicion took hold of her. Was he hoping to offer her a *carte blanche*? Did he want her to be his mistress?

Through her shock, her hurt, something else occurred to Harriet—an idea so ironic that she was forced to smile, albeit, through her tears. If Lord Dunford had succeeded in convincing her to become his newest mistress, who would he have chosen to design her jewelry?

Who, indeed?

Her amusement, such as it was, was short lived, for Harriet was suddenly struck by another thought, one that caused her to bolt upright, the sodden pillow tossed aside. Her jewelry business! She had come to Leicestershire to deliver the brooch in order to safeguard her reputation and her business. What she had done instead, was to jump from the cook pot directly into the fire.

If it ever became known in London that she had traveled about the countryside in the company of Lord Dunford, her reputation would be in shreds. And with her reputation gone, she could say goodbye to any future jewelry commissions.

After emitting a groan, she threw the tear-soaked pillow across the room, knocking over a pewter candlestick in the process. The item hit the floor with a metallic thud, but since the taper was not lit, Harriet paid it no heed. Instead, she pulled off her half boots, tossed them after the pillow, then lay back down on the bed, pulling the covers up over her head.

At that moment, her one wish was that she need never show her face below stairs again.

Chapter Eleven

*N*aturally, Harriet's wish was not granted. She made some excuse that evening about having the headache and not wanting any dinner, but when morning came, she knew she could not hide forever. They were not scheduled to leave Kipworth for three more days, and from past experience she knew that postponing the inevitable would not make it any easier.

Resigned to her fate, she washed herself, combed and repinned her hair atop her head, then donned her nicest frock—an apricot nainsook with a self-flounce around the hem and miniature ivy leafs embroidered on the puffed sleeves. Satisfied that she had done her best with her toilette, she went down to break her fast. Her cousins were already at the table. So, too, was a thick, hand-delivered letter, which had been placed beside Harriet's plate.

"You have another letter," Miles said the moment she entered the private dining room. "That is two in one week. How odd, for when we are in London, you do not received two letters in an entire month."

"Yes," she replied, her voice devoid of all interest, "very odd."

Lacking Miles's enthusiasm for the unexpected correspondence, Harriet merely glanced at the name and direction on the outside of the missive. She recognized the handwriting, not to mention the plain, burgundy-colored wafer affixed to the folded sheets, and because both were identical with those of the letter she had received two days ago, she had no difficulty in guessing the identity of the sender.

Now she guessed his identity! Here was irony indeed. If her heart had not felt as though some mythical giant had trod on it with his oversize feet, she might have laughed.

"Well," Miles asked, "do you not mean to read it?"

"Later," she lied, trying for a nonchalant tone.

Actually, if it would not have occasioned comment, Harriet would have pitched the sheets into the fireplace that very moment. The last thing in the world she wanted was to read more of his lordship's prevarications; so after placing her napkin over the unopened letter so she was not obliged to look at it, she returned her attention to Miles.

"At the moment," she said to the lad, "I should like to discuss tonight's assembly with your sister. And since I am persuaded you would find our conversation of no interest whatsoever, perhaps you would like to go around to the stables to see how the kittens fare."

"I should much rather go over to Lord Dunford's hunting box. Burton said they have a litter of new pups in the kennels."

His sister, having noticed the distress his suggestion brought to their cousin's face, bid the lad take himself off. "That is, if you have finished breaking your fast."

"I am finished," he said. "In fact, I could not eat another bite." The boy's statement notwithstanding, he grabbed up two currant buns before he left the table. One of the buns he stashed in his jacket pocket as insurance against starvation at some later hour of the morning, and the other he began devouring even before he exited the room.

The instant he was out of sight, Anna asked if she might serve Harriet from one of the half-dozen covered dishes on the sideboard. "I can recommend the buttered eggs and the kippers."

Shuddering with distaste, Harriet said she wanted nothing save a cup of hot chocolate.

The chocolate pot was within Anna's reach, but she ignored it. Instead, she left her chair and went to kneel beside her cousin, taking both Harriet's hands in hers. "What is amiss, Cousin?"

"Amiss? Why nothing is—"

"I pray you, do not attempt to fob me off with some taradiddle. Not this time. I have eyes in my head, and I know when a person has spent the better part of the night crying into her pillow. Has your distress anything to do with Mr. Randolph?"

Harriet eased her hands from her cousin's grasp. Then, thinking it better to have the unpleasant revelation over with as quickly as possible, she said, "There is no Mr. Randolph. There never was."

Anna stared, understandably confused. "I cannot have heard you correctly, for I thought you said—"

"There is nothing wrong with your hearing, my dear. The simple truth is that Mr. Randolph is none other than Lord Dunford."

"What!"

"Your Uncle Freddy was in the right of it, for the man who accompanied us to St. Agnes's Church was his lordship. Your uncle insisted that it was so, but at that time I refused to believe him.

"And now," she added, closing her eyes against a most unpleasant thought, "as if the heartache and the mortification I feel are not sufficient retribution, I shall be obliged to endure all manner of lectures from Frederick Gwynn regarding the gullibility of females my age."

"But you did nothing wrong."

"Unfortunately, that fact will weigh little with your uncle."

Suddenly angry, the young lady said, "My uncle is an imbecile!"

"Anna!"

"Well, I am sorry, Cousin, but it is the truth, and I see no reason why you should be the recipient of lectures from him or anyone else."

Anna glanced toward the door, as if to assure herself that they were still alone. "I am excessively fond of my uncle, but the simple fact is that he is not needle witted. You are far cleverer than he is, and he knows it. Therefore, if you do not admit to having been deceived by Lord Dunford, then Uncle Freddy will never know for certain that it happened. Thus, he will be unable to reproach you for anything."

There was logic to the argument, and Harriet wanted to believe it. Unfortunately, there were more people to be considered than just Frederick Gwynn. "But what of Miss Shaw, and those of the guests who saw me with his lordship?"

"You owe Miss Shaw nothing. And should she, or any of the nosy old cats who have been spying on us, be so rude as to mention Lord Dunford to you, you have only to blink your eyes, act just the least little bit perplexed at their comments, and say something like, 'Oh, is *that* Lord Dunford? How very interesting.' "

Surprised at the sensibleness of her young cousin's advice, Harriet said, "How did you become so wise?"

"Goose," Anna said, giving her cousin a hug, "from observing you."

After the cousins embraced, Anna returned to her chair and poured Harriet the hot chocolate she had asked for earlier. While she passed her the cup and saucer, she asked about the letter. "It is from his lordship, is it not?"

Harriet merely nodded.

"Do you mean to read it?"

"I do not."

"Perhaps you should. It could be that he has explained everything in his letter. It is certainly thick enough."

"I want none of his explanations. The time for them has passed. They would have been better said three days ago."

"But, Cousin, I saw how he looked at you, and the way you looked at him. I am persuaded he—"

"Please," Harriet said, the shakiness of her voice revealing just how close she was to another bout of tears, "let us speak no more of the matter. It is over. Finished."

Anna looked as though she would like to protest, but Harriet stopped her by reintroducing the subject of that evening's assembly. "I know I promised that you could attend, my dear, but you must see that I cannot accompany you."

"And what will you do instead? Hide out in your bedchamber? Would you have Lord Dunford believe that you are nursing a broken heart?"

Harriet shook her head. "I could not bear it."

"Then you must at least put in an appearance this evening. Especially since you have let it be known that you meant to attend."

"You are right, of course, but I cannot remain for the entire evening."

"As to that," Anna said, "we need stay but one hour. After that, I will say that I have the headache, and you, being the compassionate person that you are, will insist upon accompanying me to my bedchamber."

"Just the one hour?"

"Not much longer. Once we have quit the assembly room, you may return to your bedchamber and forget all about my uncle, Miss Shaw, and every nosy old tabby who ever set foot in the Rose and Crown.''

Harriet nodded, as if to say that she would do as Anna requested. The plan was good. Unfortunately, it contained one very basic flaw: After she forgot about all those other people, how was she to forget the man who had broken her heart?

"You've broken it, miss," Lucy said.

Harriet stared at the pretty ivory and lace fan. As the time for the assembly drew nearer, she had grown increasingly nervous. Needing something to occupy her hands while she waited for the maid to finish arranging Anna's hair, she had begun opening and closing the delicate semicircle. Only when she heard the unmistakable snap of one of the delicate slats did she realize what she had been doing.

"What a pity, miss. You want I should run next door to your room and see can I find another?"

Harriet shook her head. What was the point? As tightly wound as her emotions were at that moment, she would probably break the next fan as well. Besides, all she wanted to do was go above stairs, get through her allotted hour, then make her escape.

"You look a picture," Lucy said, when Anna finally rose from the dressing table. "You, too, miss," she added, including her employer in the compliment.

What the maid said of Anna was true, for the willowy girl with the silver-blond hair and eyes as blue as a Siamese kitten's, had never looked lovelier. Lucy had attached a sheer white overskirt to Anna's pale blue sarcenet dinner dress, rendering it more formal, yet suitably demure for a young girl's first evening of dancing. Not that it mattered. When a girl was as beautiful as Anna Gwynn, few people noticed what she wore.

As for Harriet, she had declined any additions to her own honey-colored dinner dress. The square neck of the two-year-old georgette was a bit daring, revealing the rounded swell of her breasts, but tonight she left off the lace fichu she usually wore and adorned the dress with a chased silver necklace. Her own creation, the simple, half-moon design of the jewelry added a subtle elegance to her ensemble.

"Lucy is correct," Anna said. "You look quite lovely."

"I do not feel lovely. I feel like a sacrificial lamb being offered up on the altar of propriety. I just wonder who will be the first to come forward, happy to light the fire that will scorch me?"

"Courage," Anna said, touching her cheek to her cousin's. "An hour has but sixty minutes. Not even Prinny himself can order it longer."

"For which," Harriet said, "I am most sincerely grateful."

Anna took one final glance in her looking glass, and as they quit the bedchamber and climbed the stairs to the third-floor assembly room, it occurred to Harriet that her cousin's eyes were bright with excitement. This was the girl's first adult evening party, and by all rights she should be looking forward to hours of dancing and pleasant conversation. Instead, she was being obliged to limit the experience to one hour.

Here, then, was another sin to be laid at Lord Care-For-Naught's door.

To Harriet's relief, when she and Anna entered the long, narrow assembly room, his lordship was not yet among the forty or so handsomely attired guests. The dancing had already begun, with the music provided by two surprisingly gifted violinists, and half the people in attendance were already engaged in a rather lively Scottish reel. The remainder of the guests stood about in small groups, or sat in chairs that lined the far wall.

Though Harriet and Anna were unacquainted with any of the other guests, in circumstances such as these, where the company was understandably thin, a certain relaxation of the formalities was permitted. For that reason, when the master of ceremonies, who introduced himself a Squire Thrumby, asked if he might present a partner to Anna for the next set, Harriet gave her permission.

The partner, a Mr. Vickers, was a painfully thin, red-haired young man who had only just completed a course of study at Cambridge. Though he appeared dazed, as if he could not believe his good fortune in securing such a beautiful partner, he bowed politely over Harriet's hand. "An honor to make your acquaintance, Miss Watson."

She did not bother correcting him. What difference did it make what he called her? Especially when in exactly fifty-seven minutes she would be on her way back to the privacy of her bedchamber.

Mr. Vickers and Anna were taking their places for the cotillion when Harriet spied Miss Eunice Shaw, who was seated with one of the other inn guests. Obviously, the heiress had been waiting to catch Harriet's attention, for she waved her fan, motioning for her to join them.

At any other time, Harriet might have pretended she had not seen Miss Shaw. In this instance, however, she was more than happy to be summoned, for Lord Dunford and his brother had just entered the room. Freddy Gwynn must have met them in the corridor, for he had engaged his lordship in conversation and was, apparently, in no hurry to allow him to escape.

Hoping to put as much distance as possible between herself and Lord Dunford, Harriet made her way along the outer edges of the long, narrow room, being careful to avoid colliding with the dancers. The air was already unpleasantly warm from the tapers burning in the wall sconces and the exertions of the dancers, and as Harriet drew near Miss Shaw, she realized why the heiress had chosen that particular spot. Ever a practical person, Eunice Shaw had claimed a chair beneath the one open window.

"Good evening, Miss Wilson."

"How do you do, Miss Shaw?"

"Me? I am quite well," she said, opening her fan and waving it back and forth, stirring up a slight breeze. "Though I understand that you were indisposed last evening. Since you are in excellent looks at the moment, I am persuaded the malady could not have been too very serious."

"A touch of sun, ma'am. Nothing more."

"Ah, yes," she said, stealing a quick look toward the door, where her intended still held Lord Dunford captive, "I seem to recall Sir Miles mentioning something to his uncle about an outing to Bosworth Field."

At this, the guest sitting beside Miss Shaw gave up all pretense of minding her own business. "You were the guests of Lord Dunford, were you not?"

Here it was at last. The gauntlet was dropped, and Harriet must either accept the challenge or crawl away a coward. For just a moment she hesitated; then, after reminding herself that avoiding an issue never made it disappear, she squared her shoulders and smiled sweetly at her nosy inquisitor. "Our party consisted of both his lordship and Mr. Burton Dunford, the gentleman's younger brother.

"In fact," she added, pointing toward the doorway, "both gentlemen are with Mr. Frederick Gwynn at this very moment. Mr. Gwynn, as you may already know, is the uncle of my cousins. He and Lord Dunford have been acquainted for some time."

As if to underscore her boredom with that particular topic of conversation, Harriet raised her fan to her lips to cover the yawn she could not suppress. Once the feigned yawn had run its course, she called Miss Shaw's attention to the dancers. "Have you seen Anna this evening, ma'am? She looks quite pretty, if I do say so myself."

The heiress did not even glance toward the moving couples. Instead, she continued to look directly at Harriet. "One who would call Miss Anna Gwynn pretty would refer to the Thames as a pond."

The analogy was apt, and this time when Harriet put her fan to her lips, it was to hide a smile.

"Furthermore," Miss Shaw continued quietly, after glancing to her right and finding the other guest in spirited conversation with one of the local ladies, "since only a fool would fail to realize that you are desirous of turning the discussion away from a certain gentleman, I will oblige you by cooperating."

"Thank you, ma'am."

"Not at all. Believe it or not, Miss Wilson, I mean you no harm." She lowered her voice even more. "In fact, once my own future is secure, and we are family, so to speak, I shall do all within my power to see that you and Miss Anna are suitably—"

Spying something, or someone, across the room, the heiress closed her fan with a snap. "Drat!" she said.

Surprised by the unladylike utterance, Harriet looked toward the door. Freddy Gwynn and Lord Dunford were still there, but Burton was gone, and in his place stood a robust-looking man in cream-colored knee britches and a puce satin coat. Probably in his mid-sixties, the newcomer was as striking a man as Harriet had ever beheld—tall and straight and commanding attention even at a distance.

His nose put Harriet in mind of an eagle's beak,

but even that amazing appendage was eclipsed by the most magnificent mustache she had ever seen. Thick, and waxed so stiff that it resembled nothing so much as oxen horns, it must have measured at least six inches on either side. Like the impressive mane of hair on the man's head, the mustache was snow white, and it quivered noticeably when he talked. As it happened, the "horns" were practically dancing at the moment, for the man appeared to be in some sort of heated discussion with Freddy.

"Who is that?" Harriet asked.

Miss Shaw sighed. "It's my da. I might have known he would find me, and me still without Freddy's ring on my finger."

Harriet was not the only person to notice what appeared to be a contretemps, for several of the people who were standing about had forsaken their own conversations and turned to stare at the two men. "Forgive me, Miss Shaw, but from here it looks as if your father and Freddy might be arguing."

"Most likely," the heiress replied, resignation in her voice.

Not a little surprised, Harriet said, "But I had not thought they were acquainted."

"Previous acquaintance is of no significance to my da. He argues with everyone."

From the increased movement of that awesome mustache, Harriet could well believe the man had practice at wrangling.

"I'm just praying," Miss Shaw continued, "that Freddy doesn't do something foolish."

A sudden vision of the fastidious and easygoing Freddy Gwynn engaging in fisticuffs obliged Harriet to turn a chuckle into a cough. "I am persuaded, ma'am, that we need not fear the argument resulting in exchanged blows."

"Blows! Freddy? Good heavens, no." The expression on Miss Shaw's face was so incredulous that Harriet resorted to more coughing.

"My worry," the heiress said, "is that Freddy might try to turn Da's attention by introducing him to Lord Dunford."

At the mention of his lordship, Harriet's amusement evaporated. "Would that be so bad?"

"Disastrous. You may take my word for it. Just let Homer Shaw discover there's a baron in our midst, and he'll move heaven and earth to see can he talk his lordship into making me an offer."

Making her an offer!

The idea was ludicrous. Unfortunately, since a not-too-dissimilar notion had recently played havoc with Harriet's heart, not to mention her emotions, she felt the heat of embarrassment creep up her neck to her face. All that prevented her from fleeing the room in mortification was the knowledge that she would be obliged to push her way past the man who had played the major part in her own self-deception.

The heiress's fears notwithstanding, Harriet doubted that a request for Miss Shaw's hand was imminent. Especially since the mine owner had just said something to which Lord Dunford had obviously taken instant exception. To the surprise of at least half the occupants of the room, his lordship answered the older gentleman's remark by grabbing the lapels of the puce evening coat and shaking the wearer in a manner not unlike that of a terrier shaking a rat.

Lord Dunford was a different man entirely from the amicable Freddy Gwynn, and since neither Harriet nor Miss Shaw had the least idea what the younger gentleman might do if sufficiently provoked, the two ladies moved as one, pushing their way through the startled dancers.

*　　*　　*

Rand had spied Harriet the instant he entered the assembly room, and if that idiot Freddy Gwynn would only go away and quit hanging on his sleeve, he meant to go directly to the lady to claim his dance. By now she had had time to read his letter through a dozen times, and he desperately wanted to know her reaction. Had she understood his motives and forgiven him? Or was she still incensed at his deception?

He hoped she was not still angry, but if she were, it would be his pleasure to coax her out of the sullens. As beautiful as she looked tonight, no man with blood in his veins would refuse the challenge.

Even at a distance he could see that she was in exceptionally fine looks. Dressed in a simple gown of honey-colored georgette, topped off by a silver necklace most likely of her own design, she was easily the most elegant woman in the room.

Rand had no idea when it had happened, but at some point during their brief acquaintance, he had come to regard Harriet Wilson as the most beautiful woman he had ever met. And if he had the dressing of her, and could send her to one of the premier mantua makers in town, there would not be a lady in the entire country to rival her. With her beauty and good taste, backed by his money, she—

"Harriette Wilson?" he heard the odd-looking fellow next to him say in response to some comment from Freddy Gwynn. "You don't say so."

Rand had no idea who the man was, presumably some friend of Gwynn's, for he had simply walked up and begun talking. From the looks of him, with his shock of snow-white hair and that preposterous mustache, the blustering fellow obviously expected people to move aside when he entered a room. Probably the local squire. Not that it mattered to Rand. He was just glad that someone else had come along to free him from Gwynn's clutches. With the mention of Harriet's name, however, his interest was caught.

"From London?" Oxen Horns asked.

"Why, yes," Freddy replied. "She resides in Town."

"We *are* talking about the same person, are we not, sir? I asked about the very pretty female with the dark brown hair. The one wearing the unusual silver necklace."

"And I told you," Freddy replied, as if speaking to one lacking in sense, "she is Miss Harriet Wilson."

"Well, now! I'll admit to being surprised, for she's a pretty thing. And quite refined looking. Nothing common or brassy about her, I'll give her that." He paused for a moment before continuing. "Though how the deuce my daughter came to be conversing with the most notorious whore in London, I vow I don't know."

"Your daughter!" Freddy gasped. "You are Eunice's father?"

Unfortunately, Freddy received no reply, for Lord Dunford, like one demented, had grabbed Homer Shaw—the wealthy mine owner Freddy hoped would soon be his father-in-law and financial savior—and was shaking him within an inch of his life.

"Shut your mouth!" Dunford muttered very close to Homer Shaw's ear, "or your age will not protect you from my wrath."

Freddy was aghast at this turn of events. Though never a man given to physical displays, he felt he must do something. Catching Lord Dunford's arm, he tried with all his might to free the startled Mr. Shaw from the younger man's clutches. "Dunford!" Freddy said. "This will not do at all. You must let him go. Stap me, old fellow, but this is very bad *ton*."

Though Dunford stopped shaking Homer Shaw, he did not release him. "Please, my lord. I beg you to desist, for this man is my future father-in-law."

The two combatants spoke at the same time; the younger one with surprise, the other with obvious delight.

"Your father-in-law!"

"He's a lordship?"

Though still in Dunford's grasp, the mine owner looked over his shoulder at Freddy. "You're certain he's a peer?" At Freddy's nod, he said, "What sort of lord is he?"

"A baron," Freddy replied, still attempting to extricate the white-haired gentleman from Dunford's grasp.

By this time, Eunice had made her way across the room, much to Freddy's relief, with Harriet right behind her. Thank heaven! They were both clever females, and between the two of them they should be able to straighten out this very embarrassing mix-up.

At Harriet's arrival, Dunford seemed to snap out of his obvious dementia and released Eunice's father.

"Da!" Eunice said. "What have you done?"

"Obviously more than you," replied her unrepentant father, straightening his mussed lapels, "for I've met a baron."

As if the previous few minutes had never happened, Homer Shaw bowed politely to Dunford. "Pray, allow me to make you known to my little girl, my lord." Pausing only a moment, he turned to Freddy once again. "What did you say the baron's name was?"

"Dunford! Not that it matters, sir, for it is me—I—Frederick Gwynn, who wishes to marry your little . . . that is, your daughter. If you recall, I sent you a letter, and—"

"Nonsense," Homer Shaw said, waving a negligent hand toward Freddy, as if brushing away a bothersome gnat. "Why would Eunice marry a mere mister if she can have a baron?"

"But she cannot have him!" Frustrated, Freddy

added, "What I mean is, Eunice wants to marry me. Quite fond of each other actually. Besides, Lord Dunford is spoken for. Been dangling after my niece, Miss Anna Gwynn, this week and more."

"He has not!" Burton Dunford said, materializing as if from nowhere just at Freddy's elbow. "Rand has no interest in Miss Gwynn, nor she in him."

"You are mistaken," Freddie said, "for I have it on good authority that he—"

"Miss Gwynn is a beautiful young lady," Burton said, "and all who know her must admire her. But it is Miss Wilson my brother wants."

"What!"

This last was spoken in unison by Harriet, Freddy, and Mr. Shaw, and as sometimes happens, a sudden and complete silence followed their surprised reaction. The entire assembled company seemed to be holding its collective breath. The dancers had long since given up any pretense of dancing, and now the two musicians laid aside their violins, the better to hear what was being said.

Unfortunately, the Homer Shaws of the world are not intimidated by a bit of silence. "But his lordship can't marry *her*," the mine owner said, his contemptuous gaze dismissing Harriet as though she were a shelf of shopworn goods.

"And why not?" Burton asked, his tone frosty enough to chill champagne.

"He just can't, that's all. Oh, she's a pretty enough piece," Shaw said. "I'll grant you that. But for all her good looks and apparent refinement, she's still a courtesan. And barons don't marry women who are for hire to the highest bidder."

A gasp went down the length of the room, though not a person spoke. Presumably, no one wanted to miss a word of the farce that was being enacted.

To Freddy's horror, Lord Dunford grabbed Homer

Shaw once again by his lapels. "You old fool," Dunford said. "The lady is not *that* Harriet Wilson."

Into the hush that followed this newest revelation, the door to the assembly room opened once again, and all eyes turned to stare at the fashionably dressed couple who entered. He was a dark-haired, dark-eyed gentleman of perhaps forty, and she was an apparent highflier whose beauty owed much to the artful application of rouge and powder.

"*Mesdames et messieurs,*" the gentleman said, making a graceful bow to one and all. "I bid you, *Bon soir.*"

"De la Croix!"

"My lord," the Frenchman said, nodding to Rand. "What a pleasure to see you again, *mon ami.* And what a surprise to find you here, of all places. The world is small, *n'est pas?*"

Dunford's eyes narrowed to cold, gray slits. "Much too small."

While the two men glared at each other, the hatred crackling between them like bolts of lightning flashing from sky to land, Sally Chadwick caught sight of Harriet, who stood scarcely six feet away. "You!" she screamed, pointing an accusing finger. "You thought you would get away with cheating me, didn't you? Well, I'm here now, and I want my brooch, you thief!"

Chapter Twelve

"Cousin!" Miss Anna Gwynn said, attempting to push her way through the crowd of titillated gawkers. "I have the headache!"

"At last," Harriet said.

Rand had only to look at her to understand the inappropriate reply. She was in shock. Her face was ashen, and her lips trembled noticeably, and if he knew anything of the matter, she was struggling to keep her eyelids wide lest she blink and start a river of tears coursing down her cheeks.

"Please," he said, stepping over to her and slipping his hand beneath her elbow, "allow me to see both you ladies safely to your rooms."

She did not even look his way. Instead, she slipped her arm from his grasp, then mumbled something about escorting her young cousin herself. The words spoken, she turned and hurried from the assembly room, forgetting completely the girl she was to escort.

Mortified beyond belief, Harriet lifted the hem of her skirt and ran down the stairs to the second floor. Though she moved as quickly as possible, Rand caught up with her at the end of the dimly lit corridor, just outside her bedchamber door. "Miss Wilson. Harriet. Please, wait."

Obviously aware that she had no intention of obeying his request, he reached around her and grasped the door latch with his left hand, holding it securely. Harriet, not wishing to cause another scene, remained perfectly still, her face to the door and her back to her tormentor. "Surely you have embarrassed me enough for one evening," she said, her voice thick with unshed tears. "I pray you, let me pass."

He did not do as she asked. Worse yet, he slipped his right arm around her shoulders and pulled her against him, her back flush against his rock-solid chest. "Harriet," he whispered, his warm breath teasing a wispy curl at her temple. "You must know that I never meant for any of this to happen."

Held so close against the length of him, she could feel his hard, muscular frame, and though she called herself all kinds of a fool, she positively ached to relax against him, to have him wrap his strong arms around her and hold her as though she were special to him. As special to him as he had once been to her.

As if he read her thoughts, he put both hands on her shoulders and turned her so she faced him. When she did not resist, he slowly slid his hands down her back, then drew her close once again, his arms enfolding her just as she had wanted. Only one brace of candles lit the corridor, and in the dim light, Harriet studied the hard, uncompromising jawline of the man she loved.

Yes, heaven help her. She loved him still!

He was so strong, so handsome—a man any woman would love. While she let her gaze travel over his entire face, Rand's gray eyes never left her mouth. And finally, as she knew he would, he bent his head and claimed her lips.

On the instant, she was lost in the warmth and passion of his kiss. With her heart pounding madly against her ribs, she felt her limbs lose their power to bear her weight, forcing her to lean against him for support. The moment she relaxed, he deepened the kiss, and eons later, when he lifted his head, Harriet was weak with sensation.

She could not move. She could not breathe. All she could do was feel, delighting in his every caress.

Softly, mesmerizingly, he kissed the corners of her mouth. Not content with that, he trailed warm, sensuous kisses down her throat, then continued along her neck until he found the pulse that throbbed wildly just behind her earlobe. Only when he dipped his head lower, to leave a warm, moist kiss on the slightly exposed curve of her breast, did she recall that this man was a practiced seducer.

Though she ached to feel his lips on hers once again, longed to surrender to the primal need churning deep inside her, somehow she found the strength to place her hands against his chest and push away, obliging him to release her from his embrace. "Would you seduce me right here in the corridor?" she asked. "Ruin me completely? Was that part of your plan?"

Rand appeared surprised by the question. "My plan?" He smiled then, as if amused by her naïveté. "Harriet, my sweet, you cannot believe that this was all some well-laid scheme to get you in my power? Acquit me of that at least. I followed you merely to offer what comfort I might."

She stiffened. Had he kissed her out of pity? Heaven help her, she prayed not. She could endure anything but that.

Though she felt very close to tears, pride came to her rescue, keeping her eyes dry and her back ramrod straight. "Has it occurred to you," she asked, "that I would not have needed comforting had you not exposed me to an entire room filled with people? Had you behaved like a gentleman, instead of the care-for-naught you are, none of this would have happened."

"But that old fool thought—"

"I know what he thought. By now, the entire village knows what he thought. Though why you must cause a scene over it I cannot even guess. After all, you jumped to that same conclusion yourself when we first met."

"Guilty as charged. But I never—"

"You never what?" she said. "You never lied to me? You never tricked me into believing you were someone you are not? You never broke my heart?"

Wishing she had not said that last part, she pushed the door open, then reached inside to the little table where she had left the letter Rand had sent around that morning. "Here," she said, placing the unopened missive in his hand. "Take your lies, both written and spoken, and go away. Leave me alone. Please. Before you rob me of what little reputation I have left."

"After last evening," Harriet told Miss Eunice Shaw, as the two early risers strolled from the Rose and Crown toward the village green, "my reputation is in shreds. And thanks to the unexpected arrival of Miss Chadwick and that rather sinister-looking Frenchman, I should not be surprised if I returned home to find that I had lost all my jewelry clients."

"Never," the heiress said. "If nothing else, my da will give you commissions enough to last you for years. He owes you that much."

Harriet stiffened, for she had had quite enough of atonement commissions. That was how she had come to be in Kipworth in the first place. "Your father owes me nothing."

"He does, but we will not argue the point. Especially not this morning, for I am much too happy. And I wish the entire world to share in my happiness."

Despite the ache that felt like a giant boulder lying

inside her chest, Harriet was not so unfeeling that she could not rejoice in another's good fortune. Miss Shaw, her new fiancé, and her father would return to her home in the next hour to prepare for the coming wedding. "Freddy is a very lucky man."

"No luckier than me," the heiress said, the joy in her eyes making her appear almost pretty. "And I owe it all to the bumble broth my da made of the assembly last evening. Or more accurately, I owe it to his desire to make amends for the debacle. Though I wish it had not caused you such embarrassment, Miss Wilson, it needed something this drastic to make Da give up his dream of having a peer in the family."

Dew still sparkled on the grass of the village green, and since neither Harriet nor Miss Shaw wished to soil the hem of her walking dress, the ladies remained on the pavement and admired the pretty black-faced sheep from afar. When this bucolic entertainment began to pale, Harriet and her new friend turned by common consent and began to retrace their steps. They were nearing the saddlery when Mr. Burton Dunford stepped out of the shop, beneath his arm a thin package about two feet long, wrapped in brown butcher paper and twisted at either end.

"Mr. Dunford!"

"Miss Wilson! What are you— What I mean is, I did not expect—" Realizing he was about to blunder, Burton doffed his hat and made the ladies a bow. "Good morning, Miss Wilson. Miss Shaw. How do you do?"

"We are both well," Harriet said.

"And Miss Gwynn? Has she quite recovered from her headache?"

Because Harriet did not wish to rehash any of the events of last evening, beginning with her cousin's attempt to extricate her from the scene by claiming

the headache, she quickly invited the young gentleman to return to the Rose and Crown with them. "It
will be my pleasure to offer you a cup of tea, and
if Anna is about, you can see for yourself how she
is doing."

Burton was still young enough to blush, and with
his dark blond hair and gray eyes, coloring so like
his older brother's, Harriet felt she was being given
a glimpse of Rand at nineteen. Rand when he was
still innocent and fresh faced—before he was shipped
off to Barbados like so much refuse.

"Thank you for the invitation, ma'am. I should like
to accompany you, but I have decided it is time I
returned to Oxford, and I am in the village completing a few tasks before I go. Not the least of which is
booking my seat on tomorrow's stage. That," he
added, "and this."

Blushing once again, he removed the thin package
from beneath his arm and showed the paper-
wrapped item to Harriet. "It is for Miles," he said.
"Something to help him remember his visit to
Leicestershire."

"Why, Mr. Dunford, how very thoughtful of you."

"Not at all, ma'am. It is just an old riding crop I
used when I was about his age. I had his initials put
on it."

"I know Miles will value it of all things."

At this, the young man laughed. "Actually, ma'am,
from what I know of the lad, he would much prefer
I made him a present of one of the new puppies in
the kennel. Unfortunately, the puppies are not mine
to give. The crop is. My . . . My brother gave it to
me for my sixth birthday, and for years I would not
let it out of my sight. Where I went, that riding
crop went."

Something—a touch of sadness in his voice, perhaps—prompted Harriet to reach up and kiss Burton

Dunford on his cheek. "As an only child, I envy you, sir. I should have liked to have a brother."

She was just backing away from the young man when out of nowhere a dirty-faced, dark-haired boy perhaps two or three years older than Miles crashed into her. She would have fallen if Mr. Dunford had not caught her by the arms.

"What the—" Whatever the gentleman had been about to say, the instant he saw the youth, whose outgrown, tattered clothes no longer covered his bony wrists and ankles, he clamped his jaws shut.

"Ma!" the boy wailed, his obsidian eyes looking at her in accusation. "Ye tripped me apurpose, ye clumsy cow."

"La," said the woman just behind him, "be that any way to speak in front of these ladies and this fine gentleman? Right mortifying, it be."

She did not look in the least embarrassed. In fact, had Harriet been asked for her opinion, she would have said the woman's blue eyes were filled with gleeful malice.

Fair haired, and somewhere in her early thirties, she might once have been very pretty, and might be still, if she bothered to wash her face or run a brush through her greasy hair. She smelled of stale sweat, and unless Harriet was mistaken, she had broken her fast with a cup of cheap gin. She should not be drinking, of course, for judging by the pumpkin-sized protrusion beneath her stained dress, the woman would soon give the sullen-faced boy a new bother or sister.

After bobbing a curtsy that was anything but respectful, the woman gave Burton a sly look. "Happen ye'll not recognize me, young sir, but I know ye. Ye've the look of yer brother. Not that we've seen his lordship these twelve years and more. Eh, Jess?" She cackled like a hen, though what she had said was not in the least funny.

"Anyway," she continued, "Belle Coombs is me name. Or once was. And that there's me son."

She grabbed the boy by his ear and yanked him toward her. "Mind yer manners, Jess. Say 'How-do' to yer uncle."

Chapter Thirteen

His uncle! Never!

This Harriet could not—would not—believe. Rand was not that boy's father! It was a lie. And with everything in her she longed to shake the cruel, spiteful woman until she admitted the truth.

Rand was no saint, and some of the things people said about him were probably based on fact. Though after last evening, when Harriet witnessed firsthand how quickly a careless accusation can travel a room, she was beginning to question many of the more lurid stories she had heard. Still, what this woman said was impossible to accept.

Harriet had observed Rand in his dealings with his brother and with Miles—both of whom would try the patience of a saint. Rand never seemed to lose his temper with them, and from what Harriet had seen, it was likely that he pictured himself in the shoes of both those difficult youths.

Randolph Dunford was no paragon, but he would never father a child, then abandon it to a life of poverty. Harriet knew this instinctively.

Nor would he have anything to do with a woman like Belle Coombs. Just thinking of Rand with this slatternly creature made Harriet's stomach roil. And if the look on his brother's face was anything to go by, he, too, was in danger of disgorging his breakfast.

For a moment, Burton stood as if glued to the spot. Then, as though suddenly remembering where he was, and with whom, he told the Coombs woman to be off. "You have had your bit of fun, now do not embarrass these ladies further."

"Ooh, I'm that sorry," she said, the amusement in her voice giving the lie to her words. She motioned to the boy. "Come on, Jess. We know when we b'aint wanted."

As if pleased with her day's work, Belle Coombs smiled, then pushed the boy ahead of her. With an unnecessary swishing of her expanding hips, she sauntered down the street, then disappeared into an alley between the apothecary's and the butcher's shop.

Once she was gone from sight, Burton could not think what to say. "Miss Wilson. Miss Shaw. I beg you will forgive this . . . this . . ." Embarrassment clutched at his throat, making speech impossible. Embarrassment coupled with remembered pain.

For years Burton had hated his brother for becoming entangled with Belle Coombs. Rand had been his hero, the person he admired most in the world, and he had betrayed a young boy's trust by bedding that slattern. Had it not been for Rand's liaison with Belle, he would never have been sent to Barbados, and his little brother would not have been left alone, with an uncaring father and an indifferent mother. Left with no one to take his part. With no one to love him.

Six-year-old Burton had been left with nothing to comfort him but a boy's riding crop. Still, no matter the degree of his resentment against his brother, he would never have exposed Rand's peccadilloes before Miss Wilson. And Miss Shaw, of course.

Eunice Shaw had watched the Coombs woman saunter away, her gypsy-looking son in front of her. Now here was young Mr. Dunford trying to ease the awkward situation the woman had left behind, begging hers and Miss Wilson's pardon for something that was none of his doing. Nor his brother's, if Eunice knew anything of the matter.

Having no patience with shilly-shallying, she asked the young man right out if he believed what that despicable woman had said.

"I . . . That is . . ."

"You shouldn't believe it, you know. Not a word of it. it is not true. Your brother never fathered that boy."

The young man turned red all the way to his ears, and though he was obviously mortified, she could tell from the hopeful look in his eyes that he wanted desperately to believe her. "You can trust me, you know. I have been gardening for years, cultivating hybrids mostly."

"Gardening? What has that to say to—"

"To how people look? I believe it has much to say, if you will but bear with me." When he said nothing, she continued. "I cannot tell you the principle behind it, but I know for a fact that I have cross-pollinated one white rose with another white rose season after season, and I have never gotten anything to show for it but another white rose."

Mr. Dunford blinked several times, as though trying to understand where this conversation was leading. "Ma'am, I have no doubt that you mean well, but I would really rather not—"

"Shh," Miss Wilson said. "Pray, do not be too hasty, sir. I believe I see where this is heading, and I find myself positively agog to know more about Miss Shaw's experiences with hybrid flowers."

"As any gardening enthusiast will tell you, there is much more I could say. I will, however, spare you my views on the merits of vegetable compost versus manure, for nothing is so boring as listening to someone prose on about a thing that interests only them."

"I am not at all bored," Miss Wilson said. "Nor, I

venture to guess, will Mr. Dunford be. In fact, I predict, ma'am, that he will soon be hanging on your every word."

Human enough to be gratified by their full attention, Eunice continued. "To put it as succinctly as possible, the times I have cross-pollinated a white rose with a red rose, my garden produced all manner of colors from dark red to palest pink. However, when I attempted white on white again, the result was the same—nothing came of it but white."

"And this works with people?" Miss Wilson asked.

"You will understand," Eunice said, "that I have so far restricted my experiments to flowers. However, after years of watching certain animals—humankind included—I have reason to believe that whatever principle determines the colors of the flowers also determines the colors of the higher orders."

Mr. Dunford regarded her with something akin to awe. "So you are saying, ma'am, that Belle Coombs—"

"A fair-haired woman with blue eyes . . ."

"And my brother—"

"A man whose hair color, like yours, is dark blond, and whose eyes are gray . . ."

"And the boy?" he said, the words barely more than a whisper.

"Looks like a gypsy," Eunice said.

"A handsome enough lad," she added, "or he would be if subjected to a judicious application of soap and water. Still, it is my opinion that two fair-haired, light-eyed people could never have produced that dark-haired, black-eyed boy. I cannot tell you who actually fathered the lad, you understand, but I can tell you without the least equivocation that it was not your brother."

The young man stared at Eunice for some time, though she doubted he saw her. Finally, he let out a sigh that sounded as though it had been waiting a dozen years to be set free. "Then it was a lie," he said. "Rand was innocent all along. And I . . . I chose to believe the worst."

As if recalling words and scenes he wished he could erase, the young man moaned.

"Mr. Dunford?" Miss Wilson said. "You are distressed. Pray, if there is anything I can do to relieve your—"

"Excuse me," he said, oblivious to everything and everyone around him, "but I must go."

After tucking the riding crop beneath his arm, he bid them a good morning. "I have something to do," he said. "Someone's pardon to ask. And I pray I have not come to my senses too late."

Eager to get back to the hunting box before his brother went for his morning ride, Burton claimed his horse from the rear of the saddlery, then rode toward the Rose and Crown to deliver the riding crop to Miles. As it happened, he spied the boy turning cartwheels in the road just beyond the inn.

Miles Gwynn, not being of a contemplative nature, had already been up to some sort of mischief, for his shirt hung outside his nankeens, his boots were covered in dust, and his hands and face were one continuous smut. "Been climbing down badger setts?" Burton asked.

Miles laughed. "If I could find one, I might give it a try."

"No, no, old fellow. Definitely a bad idea. The badger would not like it, and neither, I am persuaded, would you."

The boy gave him a look that said he would be willing to discover that fact for himself. "Actually," he said, "I have been up in that service tree over there, surveying the area as I feel certain someone in

King Richard's army must have done. Looking for a likely battle site."

"Which puts me in mind of something, General. This is for you."

Eyeing the item wrapped in the butcher paper, Miles said, "What is it?"

"Something meant to remind you of this past week, and to mark your visit to Bosworth Field."

"By Jove!"

As he might have expected, Miles was pleased to accept the gift. In his exuberance, the boy tore open the paper and removed the woven leather crop. "By Jove," he said, turning the crop over in his hand, marveling at its workmanship. "It is first-rate."

"I thought you might like it, so I took the liberty of having your initials affixed."

Miles examined the small brass plate; then, his eyes alight, he assumed a fencing position and slashed the crop through the air like an épée. *Whoosh, whoosh, whoosh.* "Bang-up to the mark," he said, abandoning his swordman's stance. "Thank you, Burton. I shall keep it always."

The two shook hands; then Burton remounted and left for the hunting box, the gray moving at a smart trot. He had not been gone above a minute when Miles, pretending to be mounted on one of the splendid Dunford hunters, took off down the road at a brisk pace, making galloping noises with his tongue and hitting the air behind him with his new riding crop, as if spurring on an imaginary steed. He had covered perhaps half a mile when he noticed something rather odd looking happening in the lane up ahead. A large tree limb lay across the road, presumably obstructing the path of an old farm wagon hitched to an equally old, sway-backed horse.

Two rather rough-looking men, both dressed in nondescript workmen's smocks and breeches, stood beside the wagon. One of the men was of average height, but the other, a giant of a man with hands the size of hams, appeared plenty husky enough to move the limb. Not that he bothered to do so. Instead, he and his companion were busy securing a canvas cover to conceal the wagon's cargo.

Under normal circumstances, Miles might have been only moderately interested. In fact, he might even have offered to lend the workmen a hand, had he not also spied Burton's horse at the side of the lane. Of Burton Dunford there was no sign. The handsome gray stood alone, pawing the ground nervously, and once the men had finished securing the canvas, the smaller fellow slapped the animal on the flanks, sending him galloping across the fields.

Perceiving right away that something sinister was afoot, Miles crouched down beside the hedges where he was less likely to be seen, then watched while the smaller man climbed aboard the wagon, taking the swayback's ribbons. "Pee-yare," he said, motioning toward the limb, "clear that away."

The giant, apparently not at all pleased to be given orders, muttered his displeasure in a language that Miles thought sounded rather like French. "Go on, ye big idgit," the other man said, "afore someone comes along and glims a look at us."

After glancing around him as if checking to see if anyone was watching, the man called Pierre lifted the end of the large tree limb as though it weighed no more than a couple of stone, and began dragging it to the side of the road.

Under cover of the noise from the limb scraping the ground, Miles scurried toward the rear of the wagon, where he pushed aside a couple of inches of the canvas. All he saw was part of a well-made top boot encircled by a bit of rope, but it was enough to convince him that what he suspected was true. Those men had abducted Burton Dunford.

Moments later, the man called Pierre climbed

aboard the wagon, and the driver slapped the ribbons against the ancient horse's rump. Slowly, the wagon wheels began to turn. Miles, thinking only that he must do something before it was too late, pushed aside the corner of the canvas and dove underneath.

Once the wagon had made its way around the bend in the road, there was nothing left to indicate that anything untoward had occurred. Nothing save a boy's braided leather riding crop lying in the dust, the initials M. G. engraved on the small brass plate.

Chapter Fourteen

Rand threw his leg over the chestnut's back, breathing easier now that he was out in the clean, fresh air, with the warmth of the sunshine relaxing his taut muscles. He had passed a miserable night—not surprising when one considered the events of the evening—and though it was still early, he could not wait another minute. He had to get to the Rose and Crown. He had to speak with Harriet.

Speak with her? He would be fortunate if she did not shoot him on sight. Especially after he had distinguished himself at the assembly as an ass *par excellence*.

He still could not believe the unmitigated stupidity of his actions. All he knew for certain was that the old fool with the ox-horn mustache had dared speak Harriet's name, and on the instant Rand had gone berserk. Blind with rage, he had wanted to throttle poor Freddy Gwynn's future father-in-law.

But that was not the worst of it.

Not content with manhandling a fellow old enough to be his father—an act that claimed the attention of every person in the assembly room—Rand had actually repeated the offense scarcely a minute later, thereby causing the scene that resulted in Harriet's being denounced publicly as a whore and a thief.

When she finally fled the room, he had compounded his blunders by following her down to her bedchamber, where he had taken her in his arms and kissed her as he had been longing to do for days.

Not that the regretted those kisses. Far from it, for he had never before experienced such dizzying passion, never known there could be such delight in ensuring another's enjoyment. He did, however, regret the way those intimate moments had ended, for Harriet had pushed him away. She had moved out of his arms, though he would have wagered his entire fortune that she did not want to.

Following the kisses, she had accused him of lying to her. Of tricking her into believing he was someone he was not. And of breaking her heart.

The first two accusations were true enough, and Rand would have done his best to explain his actions and apologize for them, had she not accused him of the third. Had he broken her heart? When?

To the best of his knowledge, a heart could not be broken unless the owner had entrusted it to another. Unless the owner had surrendered it in love.

In love! That idea had practically knocked him off his feet.

Was Harriet Wilson in love with him? Was that why she had kissed him with such innocent abandon? Why she had relaxed her soft, pliant body against his, permitting him to deepen the kiss until he thought he would go mad with wanting her? Why she had looked up at him with that warm, passionate glow in her eyes, the look all but driving him insane?

Did she? Could she be in love with him?

He was still reeling from the question when Harriet shoved his unopened letter into his hands, then told him to go away and leave her alone before he robbed her of what little reputation she had left. Without another word, she had slipped into her room and closed the door.

Rand might have followed her into the room had it not been for Miss Anna Gwynn, who had finally made her escape from the assembly room, and was at that moment hurrying down the dim corridor. Torn between his need to talk to Harriet, and the conviction that he might ruin all his chances if he forced his way past her closed door, Rand had put the letter in his pocket and walked away, not stopping until he had reclaimed his horse and ridden home.

Now, in the clear light of morning, he meant to get a few things straight with Miss Harriet Wilson. He wanted—no, he *needed* to know for certain if she had given him her heart. He had been a crazy man last evening; he might easily have misheard her. Perhaps she had said something that only *sounded* like "You broke my heart."

He had spent the better part of the night tossing and turning in his bed, punishing himself with recriminations and torturing himself with questions for which he had no answers. A man of action, he had decided to seek Harriet first thing.

If the truth be known, he had little experience or understanding of ladies. And even less knowledge of love. Until recently, his adult years had been spent in company with women whose actions and emotions were inextricably tied to the amount of money in his pockets. Of course, some of those women had declared that they loved him, but Rand had never taken them or their declarations seriously. Pocketbook love was no more substantial than the puffy white clouds that floated across a summer sky. Here one minute, gone the next.

But what of real love? Did it last? Could it, as the vicars insisted, endure in plenty and in want? In sickness and in health? Could a man spend a lifetime desiring one person, and one person only?

All Rand knew for certain was that he admired and respected Harriet Wilson. And that the feelings that had begun as friendship, had somehow become fired by a passionate desire to be with her every minute. To hold her. To kiss her. To make love to her. To protect her from harm.

Was that love? He did not know. But if anyone would have the answer, it would be Harriet, for she was the kindest, the most loving person he had ever known. Not to mention the most beautiful. And the most desirable.

Such thoughts disturbed more than they calmed, and as the chestnut trotted down the crushed-stone carriageway, amid a chorus of yelping from the kennels, Rand noticed a horse and rider leave the lane to gallop toward him. Since the raw-boned horse was obviously a hired hack, and the barrel-chested man in the ill-cut coat and red vest was obviously no gentleman, Rand pulled Mercury to a halt and waited. "May I help you?"

The man touched his finger to the bill of his felt cap. "Good morning to you, sir. 'Ave I the pleasure of addressing Lord Dunford?"

"I am Dunford."

"Bill Avery's the name. From Bow Street. I was assigned the job of observing Mon Sewer Antoine de la Croix, and I've come to inform you, my lord, that the Frenchman 'as leased an 'unting box about an hour's ride from 'ere. Near a village called Market Bosworth. I've a room at a little inn called the Fox's Den, but Mon Sewer de la Croix, along with a female of the muslin company, and a minion—a rough-looking rounder who goes by the name of Pierre du Lac—are all staying at the box. And if I ever saw a pair up to no good, my lord, it's them two Frenchies."

Knowing that he needed to hear everything Avery could tell him about de la Croix, Rand took the runner up to the house. After ordering a tankard of home brew for his guest, he led him to the billiards room, where they discussed how best to handle the Frenchman's sudden appearance in Leicestershire.

"Someone shot at me a few days ago," Rand said, "and it occurred to me at the time that the culprit might be de la Croix."

"Could be, my lord. 'E's been in Leicestershire since the early part of the week." The runner took the first sip of his ale. "If you'll forgive me asking, sir, 'as the mon sewer got a reason for wishing to see you dead?"

Rand nodded. "While in Barbados, I won a sum of money from de la Croix in a legitimate game of whist. For reasons of his own, however, he convinced himself that he had been cheated."

"A sore loser, eh?"

"You could say that."

"Rumor 'as it," Avery said, "that you won a bit of the ready from a gentleman or two at White's, and a small fortune from another at Boodle's. Played with clever gentlemen, so I 'ear. Ones as know the rules of play and pay."

"As you say, those were gentlemen."

"Which the Frenchie is not."

"Which the Frenchman is not. As you may know, de la Croix is both a pirate and a slave trader. What you may not know is that he believes I besmirched his honor, or what passes for honor in that twisted mind of his. He has vowed to be revenged on me, and as long as he is in England, I and the members of my household are in danger."

At that point, Rand thought it prudent to mention that Burton had been threatened by three thugs who live in Oxford.

"The Wexham brothers," the runner said. "I've some good news there at least."

Avery finished his ale in one long, practiced swal-

low, then set the tankard on the drop-leaf games
table beside his chair. "Seems those three make an
'abit of trying to extort a bit of gelt from some of the
young gentlemen at the university. Good at making
threats and displaying a bit of muscle, are the Wexhams. So far, though, they've been all talk."

He smiled, revealing more than one gap where
teeth should have been. "One of my associates, a
'umorless sort of fellow, 'ad a wee chat with the oldest brother. Spilt his claret, I believe, then give 'im a
little something to think about other than flim-
flamming young gentlemen."

At Rand's nod of approval, Avery gave it as his
opinion that young Mr. Dunford could return to university anytime he liked. "Just advise 'im to go about
'is business, my lord, and stay as far away as possible
from the Wexhams and their tavern. 'Appen they'll
find some other poor lad to threaten."

While Bill Avery rode back to the village of Bosworth Market, to keep an eye on de la Croix, Rand
mounted Mercury once again and rode to Kipworth,
to the Rose and Crown. To his surprise, he met Harriet in the inn yard, and far from wishing to shoot
him, as he had feared she might, she was flatteringly
pleased to see him.

"Thank heaven!" she said, as he dismounted and
tossed Mercury's reins to one of the ostlers. "I
thought you would never get here."

Impulsively, she held her hands out to Rand, and
he took them in his, to offer her what comfort he
might.

He had seen her happy, he had seen her angry,
and he had seen her flushed with passion. But this
was the first time he had seen her when her pansy
eyes were clouded with worry and she was obliged
to catch her bottom lip between her teeth to stop its

trembling. Seeing fear in Harriet's eyes had the oddest effect on him, and Rand was torn between a desire to murder whoever had frightened her, and a wish to gather her in his arms and tell her that all would be well.

Before he could do either, she stepped back, obliging him to release her hands. After taking a deep breath, as if in hopes of calming herself, she said, "I did not know whether it was wisest to wait here, in case you meant to call upon me . . . us . . . or if I should hire the donkey cart and come to you."

She had been willing to come to him. Whatever was the matter, she had been willing to turn to him.

"The donkey cart?" he said, hoping to make her smile. "The situation must be dire, indeed, if you would consider trying your luck once again with that intractable beast."

To her credit, she tried to smile. Unfortunately, the effort failed miserably, and the slight movement at the corners of her pretty mouth merely reminded Rand of how much he wished to kiss her. To stop himself from acting upon that impulse, he put his hand beneath her elbow and led her to the horse chestnut tree that all but filled the side yard of the inn. "Now," he said, once she was seated on the rustic wooden bench beneath the tree, "suppose you tell me what has you so concerned."

"It is Miles. He is missing."

In a very few sentences, she explained about returning to the Rose and Crown to find her young cousin gone off on some adventure. "I thought nothing of it until Freddy and Miss Shaw and her father took their leave. At the last minute, they invited Anna to accompany them, and she was disappointed that her brother was not here to bid her good-bye. Even then, I told myself that it was some boyish escapade keeping him away."

"It might still be," Rand said softly.

She shook her head. "I did not become unduly concerned until at least two hours later, when Miles did not return for nuncheon. That is when I began to worry, for he always returns in time for a meal."

She wore a small bonnet that tied with poppy-colored ribbons, and a simple sprigged muslin frock with matching poppy-colored trim beneath her breasts and on the short sleeves, and without realizing that she did so, she began to twist round her fingers the ribbons of her bonnet. "After nuncheon," she said, "I asked one of the ostlers if he would help me search for the boy. He . . . He came back with the riding crop."

Her voice had caught on the final words, prompting Rand to unwind the ribbon from her fingers and take her hands in his. "What riding crop?"

"It was a gift from your brother."

"Well, then," Rand said, glad to have the mystery solved, "there is your answer. When I left the hunting box, Burton had not yet returned. No doubt, Miles is with my brother."

"No," she said. "That cannot be, for Mr. Dunford was in a hurry to be home." For some unexplainable reason, her cheeks turned pink. "He had something important to do."

"It cannot have been too important," Rand said, his tone containing just a touch of skepticism, "for as I said, he was still gone when I rode away."

Taking exception to his tone, she pulled her hands from his once again. "I tell you, it *was* important. I saw your brother; you did not!"

For the first time since his arrival, Rand took her concerns for her puckish cousin seriously. As well, he began to be concerned for Burton, for something had brought thoughts of Antoine de la Croix to his mind. Just thinking of Burton and de la Croix in the same sentence sent a shaft of apprehension directly to Rand's solar plexus. It would be just like the Frenchman to wreak his vengeance on someone totally innocent of wrongdoing.

"Tell me," he said quietly, "when and where you saw Burton last."

Once again her cheeks were suffused with color. "We met in the village, where he . . . where your brother exchanged words with a woman called Belle Coombs. She was accompanied by her son, and after they left us, Mr. Dunford said something about needing to make an apology, and hoping it was not too late. He rode away then, and as I told you earlier, he was in a considerable hurry."

He hoped it was not too late. Those were Burton's words, but now they played havoc with Rand's brain. *Please heaven, let them not be a prophesy! Do not let Belle Coombs and her lies cause devastation in my life once again.*

Too late. Too late.

Rand had difficulty pushing the words from his consciousness, for if de la Croix was involved in this, it could already be too late. Burton could be anyplace by now, and Miles might well be with him. The Frenchman was a slave trader. A cruel, inhuman creature impervious to the misery and heartache he caused. Furthermore, he owned his own sailing ship, and he was adept at the kidnap and transportation of his victims.

That thought had no more than occurred to Rand when he heard a carriage and pair traveling toward the inn at great speed. Something about the urgency of the approaching team sent him running to the inn yard as well. Somehow, he was not at all surprised to see Eli Porter driving the landau.

"Whoa!" the huntsman shouted as he pulled on the ribbons.

With a sense of foreboding, Rand went to the horses' heads, holding them steady while the wizened old man climbed down from the coachman's box. "Master Rand," he said, holding a note in his outstretched hand. "Just after you left, the gray came back to the stables all blown and lathered, as if he'd been running about unchecked. Master Burton weren't with him, but this were attached to the saddle. I came fast as I could, for I kenned ye would want to know what happened."

Harriet had arrived in time to hear everything Eli said, and now she put her hand on Rand's arm. "Please," she said, "read it aloud."

The fear in Rand's heart was mirrored in her eyes, and he could not deny her request. Breaking the plain wax seal, he unfolded the single sheet. The penmanship was conspicuously adorned with flourishes and curlicues, as if the writer meant to convey the impression of humor and lightheartedness. Like the writer himself, there was nothing amusing about the message.

" 'My lord,' " Rand began, the words all but sticking in his throat, " 'while at the assembly last evening, I was visited by a most intriguing idea. Antoine, I said to myself, *Monsieur la baron* learned so much while laboring in the cane fields, *n'est pas?* Would it not be amusing for him to know that his young brother was reaping the benefits of a similar education?' "

Unable to stop himself, Rand muttered a string of expletives unfit for feminine ears. Without apologizing for his outburst, he took a steadying breath, then continued to read de la Croix's letter. " 'There is a gentleman in Jamaica who pays whatever fee I ask, if I bring him a pretty young boy. *Moi,* I prefer *les jeune filles,* but money is money, and I really must reclaim the amount you stole from me.

" '*Au revoir, mon ami.* I shall relay to Monsieur Burton Dunford your wishes for his safe passage and *la bon voyage.'* ''

Though Rand felt the bile rise in his throat, he read the final words. '' 'Your obedient servant, Antoine de la Croix.' ''

For a moment he said nothing, then he looked at Harriet, whose hand still rested on his arm. He was not certain how much a gently reared young lady would understand about the sort of men who purchased young boys, but from the terror in her eyes, she understood well enough about the slave trade.

"Rand?" she said, her voice weak with fear, "what are we to do?"

He did not try to convince her that Miles was not with Burton. How the boy came to be involved, he could not say, but in the deepest, darkest part of him, he knew it was true. Just as he knew that de la Croix would not pass up the chance to take on board a second lad. In the slaver's mind, young Miles would be a source of profit—nothing more, nothing less.

"I believe I know where the villain may be," Rand said. "I have had him under surveillance by Bow Street, and the runner informed me just this morning that the Frenchman had leased a hunting box in the village of Market Bosworth."

"Please," she said, "let us go there without delay." Since she went immediately to the landau and climbed aboard, there could be no doubt as to her intentions.

"You cannot go with us," Rand said. "Surely you must see that? The Frenchman is dangerous, and he is not alone. There is no way I could ensure your safety."

"I do not ask you to," she said, her tone incredulous. "I am not a child, but a woman grown, and I am responsible for my own actions as well as the consequences of those actions."

"Harriet, please. Climb down, so that Eli and I can be on our way. You can help best by getting word to that fellow who acted as master of ceremony at the assembly. I believe someone said he was also the justice of the peace for the neighborhood."

She did not move so much as a toe. "You," she said, pointing to Eli, "please be so good as to tell the innkeeper, Mr. Shimmerhorn, what has happened, and ask him to contact Squire Thrumby."

"Please," Rand said again, "climb down. Can you not see that my heart is already bleeding? I beg you, do not add to my pain by obliging me to remove you by force."

Harriet knew a moment's sympathy for the man known to the world as Lord Care-For-Naught. He cared very much—probably more than most. She understood that. Unfortunately, he did not understand her. "I am going to Market Bosworth," she said. "If you remove me from the landau, I shall run behind it the entire way."

"But—"

"I must go to Miles. Surely you see that? I will cause you no trouble, and you have my solemn oath that in every other thing I will do exactly as you bid me. But not in this."

Making one last effort, Rand reminded her that he had no guarantee that they would catch up with de la Croix in Market Bosworth. "If he has fled, I will follow him to London, if need be. I can do nothing else. Time is of the essence, and for that reason I would be unable to return you to Kipworth."

"Then we will both go to London."

Rand heard Eli gasp, and he did not need to turn around to know the old man's eyes would be wide with shock. And if Eli Porter was scandalized, Rand could just imagine the reaction of the so-called polite world.

"Only think," he said. "If you travel all the way to Town with me, your reputation will be irretrievably ruined."

"My reputation be damned!" she said. "Of what value is an unsullied name if we do not stop the Frenchman? I brought Miles here to Kipworth. Me. I am solely responsible. He is just a boy, and I put him in harm's way. How can I live with myself if we do not save him?"

Chapter Fifteen

They reached Market Bosworth in less than the expected hour, with Rand sitting on the coachman's box of the landau, and Harriet, riding as his passenger, holding on to the strap the entire way. Rand was skilled with the ribbons, and though he had pushed the team, they were fresh and well matched, and they traversed with ease the undulating countryside with its quickthorn hedges and woods.

Someone, Eli Porter she supposed, had shown the presence of mind to stow a set of carriage pistols beneath the forward seat, and as Rand slowed the team at a surprisingly seedy-looking inn called the Fox's Den, Harriet bemoaned her lack of knowledge about firearms. At the moment, skill with pistols was a talent to be desired.

A suspicious-looking ostler peeped around the door of the stables, as if not certain what to do with a gentleman's carriage. At Rand's signal, he came forward, moving at a rather slow pace, and went to the horses heads. "Walk them," Rand said, tossing the fellow a coin. "We will not be staying. I wish only to ask a question of the proprietor."

From the wary look in the ostler's eyes, Harriet surmised that at the Fox's Den questions were not the preferred way to begin a conversation.

"You may as well climb down and stretch your limbs," Rand said to her. "Have a drink of water," he suggested, pointing to a wooden structure at the side of the inn, "but remain within the sound of my voice."

Harriet drew breath to argue, for she wanted to hear what the innkeeper said, but remembering that she had promised to do everything Rand bid her, she held her tongue and walked around to the well as he had suggested. To her surprise, she found a young maid of all work only a few feet from the water supply, bending over a wooden tub filled with soapy water and what looked like bed linens.

The young laundress, who was only a year or two older than Miles, was even more surprised to see the visitor, for when Harriet spoke, she startled the youngster into dropping the thick, yellowish cake soap she held, and splashing dirty wash water into her eyes. Naturally, being little more than a child, she began to cry. When she tried to dry her tears, however, she could not find a spot on her apron that was not covered in oven soot or soapy water. Harriet, her heart touched by the child's discomfort, removed her own lawn handkerchief and offered it.

"Oh, no, miss," the maid said, shaking her head so hard the overlarge mobcap she wore slipped down on her brow, threatening to cover her eyes. "It's much too nice for the likes of me. But I thank ye."

"Nonsense, my dear. Here, allow me."

After putting her finger beneath the child's chin, then turning her face up, Harriet gently blotted away the tears herself. Afterward, she folded the handkerchief and slipped it into the pocket of the dirty apron. "For the next time," she said.

The youngster beamed as if she had been given a king's ransom. Then, as if remembering her manners, she curtsied and asked Harriet if she needed anything. "If yer wishful of a cuppa, miss, I can fetch Missus Bayless, her as is the master's rib."

Harriet shook her head. "Thank you, but I am merely waiting for my friend. The gentleman and I are looking for someone who is staying at a hunting box in the neighborhood, and my friend went inside to ask directions of the proprietor."

"Yes, miss." The child bobbed another curtsy, then bent over the wooden tub once again, reaching beneath the dirty water to reclaim the soap. She had just found it when she lowered her voice, speaking so softly Harriet had to strain to hear. "You looking for the Frenchie, too?"

"The Frenchman?" Harriet's chest felt tight, as if her lungs had forgotten how to function. After drawing a ragged breath, she spoke quietly, not wanting to frighten the child. "Do you know him?"

"Me, miss? Never glimmed eyes on him. Scared of Frenchies, I am." She looked to her right, then to her left, as if to be certain that no one was listening. "A few days ago, I heard that big man what's staying here, the one with the red vest, ask the master if he knew a Frenchie."

"And did he?"

The youngster shook her head. "The master said he didn't know nuffink, but that's what he allus says when folks ask questions. 'Course, when that big man came around to the kitchen and asked the missus, she held out her hand. 'Show me your gelt,' she says, 'and I'll tell you where to find that Frenchie.' "

Her heart racing faster than an Arab stallion, Harriet asked the child if she had heard anything more.

"Yes'um. When the big man give Missus Bayless some coins, she told him the Frenchie were staying at Mr. Clive's hunting box."

"Mr. Clive's hunting box," Harriet repeated softly. "Do you know where that is?"

The child giggled as if that were a funny question. "Lived here all my life, miss."

"Of course you have. How foolish of me. So tell me, if I wished to go to there, what would be the best way?"

"That way," she said, pointing to the right. "Ye walk just a short piece, till you come to a little spinney. The gate is just past the spinney."

"Bless you," Harriet said. "I do not have any coins with me, but I shall remember you in my prayers."

The youngster was still bobbing curtsies when Harriet turned and hurried back around to the front of the inn. Before she reached the entry, Rand came out, his face looking thunderous enough to produce rain.

"I had no luck," he said. "The innkeeper knows something, I am convinced of it, but he would not be persuaded to share the information with me. Neither money nor threats loosened his tongue, and when I caught him by the collar, the better to convince him of my need, several men came in from the taproom to offer him their assistance. Thinking it best to play least in sight, I let him go and backed out of the—"

"I know where de la Croix is staying," Harriet said, unable to wait another minute. "The box is down the road a bit. Just beyond a spinney."

After a stunned silence, Rand signaled to the ostler to bring the team, and once he had tossed the fellow another coin, he helped Harriet back into the landau. Sparing a moment, he smiled at her. "Next time," he said, "I stay within the sound of *your* voice, while you do the questioning." It was as close to an apology as she was likely to get, but Harriet was too excited to quibble. She only hoped they got there in time.

The spinney was less than a mile away, on the right and as the maid had said, the gate and the carriageway were just beyond the little wood. Like many an estate where the owner never made an appearance, the place was in need of attention. The carriageway wanted regrading, and what had once been a sweep of rolling greensward leading to the house was now badly overrun with tall weeds. As well, the kennel, which was situated some distance from the stables, looked as if the roof might collapse at any moment.

"While you were gathering information," Rand said, "did your informant happen to mention whether or not the kennels here are occupied?"

"No. Why? Does it matter?"

"It could," he said. "No matter the time of day, if anyone drives up the carriageway at my box, the hounds set up a chorus of fevered barking guaranteed to warn even the least suspicious person."

"Oh, no. Then what should we do?"

"Leave the landau in the spinney," he said, "and approach the house on foot."

After tying the team to a low tree branch, where the landau could not be seen from the road, Rand checked the pistols. Finding them both loaded and ready to fire, he looked at Harriet. "I do not suppose you . . ."

"Sorry," she said. "Remiss of me, I know, but I never learned to handle a weapon. Just add it to my list of flaws."

To her surprise, he chuckled. "An ever-expanding list," he said.

Without another word, he slipped one pistol into the waist of his breeches, then slung the holster of the other over his shoulder. "Are you quite certain you want to do this?" he asked. "No one will think any the less of you if you wait with the horses."

"I would think less of me," she said.

There being nothing more to say, he tipped her

face up and kissed her, lingering just a few seconds to enjoy the softness of her lips. "For luck," he said.

"Yours or mine?" she asked just a bit breathlessly.

"Both."

After reminding her that she was to do exactly as he said, they began making their way around behind the overgrown greensward, their objective to approach the house from the rear. Moving quietly, they stayed low, using the weeds and shrubs to hide them as much as possible. They had almost reached the double-Dutch door that led to the kitchen area, when the door suddenly burst open.

Rand pushed Harriet to the ground, then shielded her body with his own. "Shh," he warned, for a man had stepped outside into the open, a medium-size trunk on his shoulder. Of average height, the man wore a workman's smock and breeches, and as far as Rand could tell, he was unarmed.

"Hey, Pee-yare," the man said. "What you reckon that light skirt'll say when she discovers there b'aint enough room in the carriage for her now, and that his nibs is leaving her and her trunks here?"

"*Firmez la bouche*," came the disgruntled reply; then a giant of a man appeared in the open doorway, a large, leather-covered sea trunk on his shoulder.

Rand recognized him immediately as the fellow he had hit with the bottle that night in Barbados. The Bow Street Runner had said that de la Croix had an accomplice, one Pierre du Lac, but he had not mentioned the third man. No matter, if Rand could somehow get him alone, he would immobilize him. That would leave only the giant and de la Croix, and Rand had two pistols—two pistols he would not hesitate to fire.

Apparently, the smaller man did not speak French, for he did not close his mouth as instructed. "When that one wakes up and finds we're gone," he continued, "she's like to cause one hell of a row. Squawk like a chicken, I'm thinking."

"Dead chickens," Pierre said. "They do not squawk."

At this, the other man stumbled and dropped his trunk. "Hey, just a minute here, Pee-yare. A bit of kidnapping's one thing, but I b'aint killing no female. Light skirt or no."

"Silence!" Pierre cautioned. "Or there will be two dead chickens."

The man's lips began to tremble, as though it had just occurred to him that he, too, was expendable. He bent to retrieve the dropped trunk, and as he lifted it to his shoulder, he looked all around him, as if searching for an escape route. "You go on to the stable, Pee-yare, and start loading his nib's trunks in the boot. I . . . I forgot sommit."

The giant, ignoring him as if he were no more than a pesky fly, merely brushed past him and continued toward the stable with his burden. Once he was out of sight, the smaller man dropped the trunk once again and began running in the opposite direction, toward the carriageway. He had gotten only as far as a stand of overgrown hawthorn bushes when he suddenly fell to the ground.

To Rand's surprise, the fellow did not get up. Instead, a pair of brawny arms reached from the midst of the hawthorns, caught the man's ankles, and dragged him into the shrubbery. Moments later, Bill Avery, the Bow Street Runner, stepped out into the open and waved in Rand's and Harriet's direction.

More pleased than he could say to know the runner was here, Rand motioned for Avery to join them. Minutes later, the three of them were crouched in the weeds, with Avery telling them everything he had discovered. "I was 'ere when they brought the wagon containing the two lads. All tied up like a Christmas goose, both of them."

At Harriet's indrawn breath, the runner touched the bill of his cap. "Begging your pardon, miss."

"No, no," she said. "Pray continue, Mr. Avery."

"With what you told me, my lord, about the mon sewer wanting revenge, and 'im being a slave trader and all, I put two and two together quick enough. With one against three, though, I thought as 'ow it'd be best if I didn't tip my 'and by trying a rescue. Knew you'd be along soon as you knew Mr. Dunford was missing."

He slid a glance toward Harriet. "Though I didn't expect you'd 'ave a lady with you."

"The boy is Miss Wilson's cousin," Rand said, leaving the explanation at that. "Tell me," he said, changing the subject, "have you a plan?"

The runner nodded. "Been thinking, my lord, now that there's two of us, that I'd enjoy going a round or two with that big fellow. I see you've brought a pistol, so if you'd like to 'ave a talk with the mon sewer, while I follow the minion out to the stables, we should 'ave everything in 'and in no time. Course, there's still an old servant in the house, and that female the mon sewer brought."

"Please," Harriet said, holding her hand out for the spare pistol, "do not give her another thought. I promise you, you may leave Miss Chadwick to me."

Not five minutes later, Harriet walked around to the front of the house, stepped beneath the sagging portico, and knocked at the scarred oak door. When no one answered, she thought she would be obliged to knock a second time, but the door was finally opened by an elderly man who looked as though he had probably been in service there for at least sixty-five years. Silver haired and stooped with age, he must also have been hard of hearing, for he held an ear trumpet in his hand.

Not wanting to shout, and perhaps alert de la
Croix that something was happening, Harriet
breathed a sigh of relief when she spotted Sally
Chadwick standing just behind the old servant, curi-
ous as to who had come calling. Obviously surprised
at the identity of her visitor, the woman's jaw went
slack. "You!"

"Yes," Harriet said, donning what she hoped was
a suitably subservient smile, "it is I. I prayed I might
find you in."

"How did you know I was here?"

Ignoring the question, Harriet said, "I have come
to rectify an egregious wrong, Miss Chadwick; so if
you would be so good as to step out here, I have
something for you."

"You have my brooch? It's about time!"

Pushing aside the old man, the woman stepped
out beneath the portico. Spurred by avarice, she paid
not the least attention when Harriet, while keeping
the contents of her right hand concealed beneath the
folds of her skirt, reached around with her left hand
and closed the door, so that the two of them were
alone. "I should not like your friend, Monsieur de la
Croix, to disturb us."

"Why should he? This does not concern him. Besides Antoine is upstairs with those two—" She
stopped herself just in time. "He is busy."

*So, the woman knows about the kidnapping. She is not
just some innocent pawn in the Frenchman's plan. She
knows, and she has done nothing to help Miles and
Burton.*

Keeping the smile firmly on her lips, Harriet
backed away from the portico, and like a lamb to
the slaughter, Sally Chadwick followed, never once
suspecting that anything was afoot. "I knew you
would come wanting to make amends, Miss Wilson,
once I exposed you before that bunch of farmers and

cits at the assembly last evening. Now where is my brooch? And it had better be the real one, or someone is going to be locked up for a very long time."

"Locked up? How interesting that you should mention incarceration, Miss Chadwick, for I have been thinking this half hour and more that those kennels would make an excellent jail."

As if unable to stop herself, Sally Chadwick turned to stare at the tumbled-down kennels. When she turned back, she gasped, for she spied the pistol Harriet held in her right hand, the barrel pointed directly at Sally's chest. "What the deuce!"

"Start walking," Harriet said. "For at least the next few hours, your new home will be the kennels."

"My new—Is this some sort of jest?"

"I should not think so. Especially since no one is laughing. Least of all the young man and boy the Frenchman kidnapped this morning."

Harriet was obliged to swallow before she could continue. "Now do as I say, and start walking. And I implore you, madam, do not do anything foolish, for neither of us would be happy if I were forced to shoot you."

The woman began to tremble, and when she took the first step, she tripped, all but falling to the ground. "Please," she said, "have you no womanly kindness?"

"Had you," Harriet asked, "when you saw two frightened lads tied up like animals?"

"Please," Sally pleaded, "do not lock me in that filthy place. Keep the brooch. I no longer want it. Just go away and leave me alone."

"I will go away soon enough," Harriet said, "but not before I see you safely locked away with the rest of the bitches. Now move!"

Chapter Sixteen

Rand entered the house through the kitchen, then waited at the end of the ground-floor corridor until he heard the knock at the front door. Once Harriet had invited Sally Chadwick to come outside, and Sally had accepted, he motioned for the ancient servant to come to him.

"Yes?" the old man said, confusion in his rheumy eyes. "Do I know you, sir?"

Noticing the ear horn, Rand leaned forward and whispered in the servant's ear. "Where is the Frenchman?"

"In the attic, sir, but I would not go up there if I were you. The fellow is no gentleman, and he has a weapon. A knife. I have seen it inside his coat."

Rand patted the old man on the shoulder, then slipped a gold coin into his hand. "Find some safe place to hide," he whispered, "and do not come out for at least half an hour. By then, I will have taken the Frenchman away, and you will have the house to yourself once again."

"Yes, sir. Thank you, sir. Thank you so much."

While the old man moved away as quickly as age and stiff bones would permit, Rand slipped off his boots, removed the pistol he had placed in the waist of his breeches, and began a slow, quiet climb up the two flights of stairs leading to the attic. The banisters were gritty to the touch, and like the rest of the property, the house was in poor condition, with brown spots along the walls where the rain had leaked through the roof.

Not that Rand cared about anything but reaching the attic and surprising Antoine de la Croix before he had time to draw his weapon. He did not wish to kill the man, but he would do so if the slave trader forced his hand. To free Burton and Miles, Rand would do whatever was necessary, and worry later about paying the price for his actions.

As he neared the top floor, he heard someone talking, and when he placed his ear to the door, he recognized his brother's voice. "Leave the boy here," Burton said. "Please."

"Mais, non," the Frenchman said. "I cannot do that."

"But you said that all you wished was to be revenged on my brother. By taking me, you will have more than reaped your vengeance. The boy has done nothing to you, and he means nothing to Rand. I beg of you, just leave him tied up here in the attic. Let the servants find him after we are gone."

Hearing his brother plead with that soulless devil infuriated Rand, and after making very sure that the pistol was cocked and ready to fire, he raised his foot and kicked in the door.

"Sacre bleu!"

De la Croix had been sitting on a battered old stool, and when he heard the door crash open, he turned too quickly and lost his balance, falling to the dust-covered floor. Losing no time, Rand moved to stand above him, his pistol pressed firmly against the Frenchman's forehead. "Move but an inch, de la

Croix, and your brains become one with the dust beneath you."

Feeling inside the villain's coat, he found the knife the man had tried to use against him all those months ago in Barbados. "And now," Rand said, "you will oblige me by turning onto your stomach, with your hands flat on the floor above your head, the fingers spread wide. Move very slowly," he cautioned, "and do not do anything to try my patience, for it would give me great pleasure to rid the world of your loathsome presence."

Knowing better than to take his eyes off the wily Frenchman for so much as a moment, Rand had not yet looked toward the two captives. "Burton?" he said at last.

"I am here."

"Are you injured?"

"A few scratches. Nothing to signify. But my hands and feet are bound behind me with rope."

"Can you move? Can you come close enough to me so that I can cut you free?"

"No. I dare not, for the rope is also wound around my neck. The slightest movement, and I will be throttled."

"Always that extra bit of cruelty, eh, de la Croix? I should have suspected as much."

Rand was filled with rage, and it was all he could do not to use the knife on the man who lay at his feet. Only just controlling the urge to retaliate, he spoke to Miles, asking the boy if he was similarly bound.

"No, sir. Just my hands and feet."

"Then can you come to me?"

As if in answer to the question, Rand heard a series of thumps as the lad slid himself across the floor. "I am here," he said at last.

Chancing a quick look to his right, Rand sliced the

razor-sharp knife through the rope, freeing the boy's hands. "Now," he said, handing the knife to Miles, "I depend upon you to finish the job."

Before the lad had succeeded in freeing himself completely, they all heard the sound of heavy boots on the stairs. "Pierre!" de la Croix yelled. *"Vite!"*

"Sorry to disappoint you," Bill Avery said from the doorway, "but your 'enchman is 'aving troubles of 'is own. Afraid 'e won't be 'elping anyone for some time to come."

Having said his piece, the runner entered the attic and took the rope that had bound Miles's feet. "Thank you, lad. I'll make good use of this." With the speed and skill of one who has performed the task many times, Avery pushed his knee between the Frenchman's shoulder blades, forced his arms back, then busied himself tying de la Croix's wrists.

When the Frenchman was securely bound, Rand passed the pistol to the runner, took the knife from Miles, then freed his brother. "Can you stand?"

"I must," Burton replied, his voice suspiciously husky, "if only to look you in the eyes like a man and ask you to forgive me."

"Silly gudgeon," Rand said, taking the younger man's arm and helping him to his feet, "there is nothing to forgive."

"But, I—" Burton began.

"There are no conditions," Rand said. "You are my brother. That is enough."

Harriet, hurrying up to the attic to see for herself that her young cousin was alive and well, arrived just in time to see Lord Care-For-Naught and his brother embrace each other for the first time in more than a dozen years.

With tears streaming down her cheeks, she opened her arms to Miles, who allowed her to hug him for a full thirty seconds. "You grubby, disgusting boy!" she said at last. "I vow, I do not know whether to kiss you or murder you."

Ignoring her quandary, the boy eased out of her embrace. "Cousin," he said, "where have you been? You missed all the excitement!"

Chapter Seventeen

London
Three weeks later . . .

*H*arriet sat at her worktable, carefully folding the precious metal prongs into place so the clear, bright emerald would be secure in its gold setting for years to come. She had been working on the betrothal ring almost from the moment she and Miles arrived at the townhouse in Marylebone, and now it was finished at last.

The commission had been waiting for her when she returned from Leicestershire, along with instructions from the unnamed client that he desired a flawless stone. The cut and the setting he would leave to her, but the emerald must never have been worn before. "Money is no object," he had written, "but I insist upon a new stone, for a new beginning."

"It is beautiful," Anna said, looking over her cousin's shoulder.

Harriet sighed, for it was, indeed the loveliest ring she had ever fashioned. "I only hope the young lady it is meant for will think it as nice as we do."

"And you still do not know for whom it is intended? Nor who commissioned it?"

Harriet shook her head. At first she had been con-

vinced that the commission came from Mr. Homer
Shaw, but when Anna returned to town three days
ago, she swore that the mine owner had been persuaded at last to abandon his plan to compensate
Harriet for the embarrassment he had caused her at
the assembly. "Although," Anna said, a dimple showing in her cheek, "the sweet old thing insists that I
am to have a string of pearls for my come-out this
spring. And he says he will not take 'no' for an
answer."

"I begin to suspect, my dear, that saying 'no' never
entered your head."

Her only answer was a quickly covered giggle. "By
that time," she said, "Eunice and Uncle Freddy will
be married, and Mr. Shaw will be my great-uncle.
Surely there can be nothing wrong with accepting a
gift from a great-uncle."

While Anna beguiled her cousin with further tales
of Mr. Shaw's marvelous house, and the suite of
rooms he was having refurbished for Freddy's and
Eunice's use following their wedding next month,
Harriet fetched a chamois cloth to buff the bright
yellow gold of the emerald betrothal ring. She had
just completed the task, and was choosing a suitable
leather jeweler's case, when the knocker sounded at
the entry door.

A minute later, Lucy came to the workroom door
and announced a visitor. "It's the gentleman from
Kipworth, Miss Harriet, and he asked if you and
Miss Anna were home."

Rand. He has come to see me at last!

On the instant, Harriet was transformed from a
sane, competent female to a certifiable idiot, one
whose fingers trembled so badly they made a hope-
less knot of the strings of her apron. Too nervous to
wait for assistance, she jerked the apron over her
head. "Drat! Now I have turned my hair into a bird's
nest. And just look at this dress," she said, staring

with loathing at the pale pink muslin. "Why, if I have worn it once, I have worn it a thousand times! I . . . I cannot let him see me like this."

"Personally," Mr. Burton Dunford said from the corridor just outside the workroom, "I find nothing to dislike in either your hair or your dress."

"Oh," Harriet said. At the sight of the young man, disappointment and embarrassment warred inside her for dominance, with embarrassment the ultimate victor. Though she would have liked nothing better than to have run from the room, she smiled at the visitor and offered him her hand. "How nice to see you, Mr. Dunford."

"Burton. Please," the young gentleman said. "I hope I have not come at a bad time."

"No, no. Of course not." All too aware that she had made a complete fool of herself, she asked Rand's brother how his studies were going. "You have returned to Oxford, have you not? I remember your saying you meant to do so. Of course, that was the day that you and Miles were—" She bit off the final word, not wanting to recall that awful day and the suffocating fear she had felt just knowing that her cousin and Burton were at the mercy of a man who was without a conscience.

Apparently, Mr. Burton Dunford had no difficulty whatever speaking of the incident, for in a very few minutes he had made the ladies current with all that had occurred since last they met. "After you left Kipworth, Miss Wilson, the Frenchman and his accomplices were taken into custody and charged with kidnapping. Except for the woman, who has already been tried and sentenced to five years at Newgate for aiding and abetting, the others are being held until they can be tried at the assizes. Following the trial, my brother believes that all three men will be transported to Australia."

Just the mention of Lord Dunford caused the heat

to rise in Harriet's cheeks. Where was he? Why had he not written to her? She had heard nothing from him since their brief good-bye the afternoon of the kidnapping, when he had helped her into the landau. Without a word, he had pressed her hand to his lips. Then, with reluctance—or so she had thought—he had bid the hired driver deliver her safely to the Rose and Crown in Kipworth.

During the two days that had followed, Harriet had haunted the window that looked onto the inn yard; all to no avail. Rand had not come. Finally, the hired chaise arrived to take them back to London, and she and Miles were obliged to leave Kipworth, with no one save the landlord, Mr. Shimmerhorn, to bid them God's speed.

Unable to stop herself, Harriet asked Burton if his brother was well.

"Never better," the gentleman replied. "He and I went down to West Sussex last week, to Ford Park. Our grandmother wanted to see us, and Rand needed to look over the place after all these years. Been giving all kinds of orders for painting and general repairs about the estate. Seems he's ready to take up residence at last. Naturally, the dowager could not be happier, for she was forever telling him it was time he settled down and began filling the nursery with little Dunfords."

Little Dunfords? Harriet caught her bottom lip between her teeth before its quiver betrayed her. Starting a family was a joyous undertaking, so why did the idea of little blond-haired, gray-eyed girls and boys running about West Sussex make her want to weep? Could that empty feeling inside her chest have anything to do with the fact that those future Dunfords would call some other woman "Mother?"

"Then his lordship will not be returning to London?" Anna asked.

"Not on a permanent basis. He and I spent a great

deal of time together, just talking and getting reacquainted, you understand, and it is my belief that he would be just as happy never to see London again."

Harriet was afraid to blink lest the moisture that suddenly pooled in her eyes should slip down her cheeks. If Rand remained in West Sussex, then she would never see him again, and she could not abide the thought of a future without him . . . without the man she loved. True, he did not love her, but if he were here in London, there was always the chance that she might meet him by accident. If nothing else, Mayfair was only a few miles' distance from Marylebone, and she would draw comfort from knowing that he was not far away.

"A ride through the park?" Anna said, bringing Harriet's thoughts back to the moment, and reminding her that she could not give way to her misery in front of their guest. "What a splendid idea. I will get my bonnet."

"What of Miles?" Burton asked. "Would he care to join us, do you think?"

"Miles is not here," Anna replied. "Our uncle took him to Eton for an interview. It is our hope that he will be a student there by next term."

"Splendid school," Burton said. "My brother and I both attended. The lad will learn a great deal there."

"Hopefully," his sister said, "he will learn to stay out of trouble!"

Somehow, Harriet maintained her composure through the next few minutes, while Anna fetched her bonnet and a wrap. As soon as the two young people left for their drive, however, she laid her head down on the worktable and gave herself up to a bout of tears that left her eyes swollen and her head stuffy. As ill luck would have it, she was searching for a handkerchief to mop away the aftermath, when a knock sounded at the front door.

Having made up her mind to have Lucy deny her,

she was surprised when Bertha came to the work-room to tell her she had a visitor. "He didn't give his name," the cook said, lowering her voice, "but he's a gentleman if ever I saw one. Dressed in the first style of elegance, and driving a curricle and pair that's bang-up to the nines, as the saying goes."

Speaking normally once again, she said, "I showed the gentleman to the front room, Miss Harriet, on account of he said he was come to see you on busi-ness. Something about that emerald ring."

The betrothal ring. Of course.

Harriet could have wished the client had chosen a better time, but considering the profit she would make from the ring, she decided it was best not to reveal her displeasure at his ill timing. Furthermore, since the ring was finished, and ready for the hand of the gentleman's fiancée, there was no reason why he should not have it right away.

Though she wished she had a few minutes so she might go up to her bedchamber and repair the dam-age done to her face and hair, she did not want to keep the client waiting. Chances were he would not even notice her appearance; after all, he was inter-ested in the ring, not in the jeweler.

"Sir," she said, opening the door that connected her workroom to the reception area, then placing the open jeweler's box on the glass display case, "I trust you will be pleased with what you see." Only when she had turned the box to her satisfaction, so that the afternoon light sparkled off the exquisite emerald, did she look directly at the tall gentleman who stood beside one of the gold damask wing chairs.

"Every time I look at you," he said, "I am pleased with what I see."

"Rand!"

Harriet could not believe her eyes. Rand was here. In her home. Scarcely an arm's length away. If she leaned forward just the least little bit, then reached out her hand, she could touch him. Oh, how she yearned to touch him.

If she did not know it to be impossible, she would have sworn that he had grown even handsomer in the three weeks since she had seen him last. Tanned from his stay in the country, he was dressed in a cinnamon-colored coat that complemented his dark blond hair, and York tan breeches that showed to perfection his powerful thighs.

"I have missed you," he said.

The soft, deep tone of his voice sent shivers through Harriet's entire body. And yet, if he had missed her, why had he stayed away so long? Unsure of herself, and needing desperately to know the answer, she said, "Why are you here?"

"Why? Perhaps because we parted too soon, and I never got to tell you how very brave you are."

Brave? She felt like the veriest coward. A watering pot without confidence or resolve.

As if reading her thoughts, he took a good look at her face. "Have you been crying?"

"Crying? Why, no I—" Drat! With the excitement of seeing him, she had forgotten about her recent bout of tears. "I must look an absolute fright."

He shook his head. "Impossible."

Though cheered by the single word, she lifted her hands to her hair, where several strands had tumbled free of the usually neat arrangement. "My hair is mussed. My dress is at least a thousand years old, and if my eyes are not red, my nose certainly will be. Deny if it you dare."

Reaching across the surface of the glass display case, which was all that separated them, he touched his fingertips to the side of her face, then gently combed back a lock of hair, tucking it into the loose knot atop her head. The simple act sent wave after wave of sensation through Harriet, obliging her to put both hands on the display case to maintain her balance.

"All you say may be true," he said, the words little more than a whisper, "and yet, you are still the most beautiful woman I have ever known. Beautiful, and brave, and generous. And," he added, leaning so close she felt the warmth of his breath against her cheek, "unbelievably kissable. In fact, for the past three weeks I have dreamed of little else but holding you in my arms and kissing you."

Her heart began to thump, for her own dreams had centered around just those same activities. Was that why he was here? To hold her? To kiss her? If so, she wished he would tell her so and end her misery.

"Why are you here?" she asked once again. The question sounded harsher than she had intended, but she would not take it back.

"Why?" He lifted the small leather box from the glass counter. "I have come for the ring."

After removing the ring from the box, he slipped the gold circle onto the tip of his little finger, then held the stone up to the window. Turning his hand first one way then the other, he watched the play of light on the emerald.

While he observed the brilliance of the gem, Harriet observed his hand as though mesmerized. It was a masculine hand, strong yet shapely, and as she remembered the soft touch of his fingers combing through her hair just moments ago she wondered how it would feel to have those strong hands caress her from head to toe.

"Exquisite," he said, as if in answer to her question.

"What?"

"The emerald. It is exquisite. Just like the lady for whom this betrothal ring is intended."

A pain sharp as any knife ripped open Harriet's heart. Rand was betrothed. And she had made the ring. Calling upon all the strength she possessed, she said, "Am I to wish you happy?"

"Wish me happy? No," he said softly. "*Make* me happy, as only you can, by telling me that you will be my wife."

She looked up, meeting those wonderful gray eyes, and the warmth she saw there stole the breath from her lungs, leaving her incapable of speech.

"Will you wear this beautiful ring," he asked, "then allow me to place another beside it? A band of plain gold?"

Yes! Oh, yes! Harriet wanted to shout her reply, to throw herself into his arms and never let him go. And yet, she could not believe this was really happening. What if she had cried herself to sleep while in the workroom, and was even now dreaming the whole? After all, Rand was a peer. Handsome and wealthy, he could have any woman in the world.

Afraid to believe, she said, "Are . . . Are you quite certain that it is me you want?"

As if not trusting his words, he caught her wrist and gently led her from behind the display case. Then, when there were no more barriers between them, he took her in his arms and claimed her lips. Softly at first, then with more insistence, he teased her lips with his own, kissing her until she lost all sense of reality, lost awareness of everything but him : . . his hard chest, his strong arms encircling her, holding her tightly.

"Rand," she said, when at last he lifted his mouth from hers, "I love you so. Please, tell me that you love me too."

"Love you?" he said, crushing her against him and holding her as though he meant never to let her go. "I adore you. Until I met you, I did not even know what love was. How could I, when I had lived for thirty years without it? And now . . ."

"And now?" she said, hope slowly banishing the last of her fears.

"And now," he said, "if I had to live just one more day without your love, I think I would surely die."

"Not one more day," she whispered. "Nor one more second."

Wanting to show him what was in her heart, Harriet placed her hands on either side of his face and gently urged his head down so that she could kiss him. Tentatively at first, she touched her lips to his eyelids, then slowly, starting at his right temple, she kissed her way down his strong jawline, across his chin, then back up to his left temple.

"Here is my love," she said. "Take it. I give it to you freely. My heart, my soul are yours. Now and forever."

Finally, when she could endure it no longer, she pressed her mouth to his.

"My sweet," he whispered against her lips, the words husky with emotion, "you still have not said that you will marry me."

Confident now that Rand loved her every bit as deeply as she loved him, and that what they felt now was only the beginning of what was to come, Harriet could no longer contain her joy. With her head tipped back so she could look into his eyes, she laughed softly. "I will marry you," she said, "but only if you are quite certain you know what sort of bargain you are making. I am not submissive, you know."

"Oh, that much I have seen for myself."

"And do you remember the donkey that was too stubborn to leave the apple trees?"

"I remember," Rand said.

"At times, when I am convinced that I am on the

side of right, I make that animal appear positively congenial."

Happier than he had ever been in his entire life, Rand was having a difficult time containing his laughter. "Not submissive. And stubborn. Is that all?"

"Just one more thing."

"And that would be?"

She hesitated for only a moment. "I, er, have been told that I sometimes snore."

At this final confession, Rand threw back his head and laughed, not stopping until he was obliged to wipe his eyes. "If you remember," he said, "when I requested the emerald for your betrothal ring, I stipulated that the stone be flawless."

"I remember."

"In a gemstone," he said, "I appreciate near perfection. In a wife, however, I believe perfection would be exhausting. I could never live up to her standards. Give me a lady with flaws every time."

"Then here I am," Harriet said, slipping her arms beneath his coat and pressing her warm, supple body close to his. "Flaws and all, I am yours for the taking."

When she turned her face up to his, her parted lips inviting his kiss, Rand knew that he was home at last.

"I love you so much," she whispered.

"And I love you," he replied. A man of action, Rand was afraid those three simple words would never express the true depth of his feelings; so he gathered her close in his arms, bent his head, and demonstrated what was in his heart.